Columbia University

Dedication of the New Site, Morningside Heights

Saturdey, the second of May

Columbia University

Dedication of the New Site, Morningside Heights
Saturdey, the second of May

ISBN/EAN: 9783337388003

Printed in Europe, USA, Canada, Australia, Japan

Cover: Foto ©Andreas Hilbeck / pixelio.de

More available books at **www.hansebooks.com**

COLUMBIA UNIVERSITY

DEDICATION OF
THE NEW SITE

MORNINGSIDE HEIGHTS

—

SATURDAY THE SECOND OF MAY

M D C C C X C V I

PROGRAMME

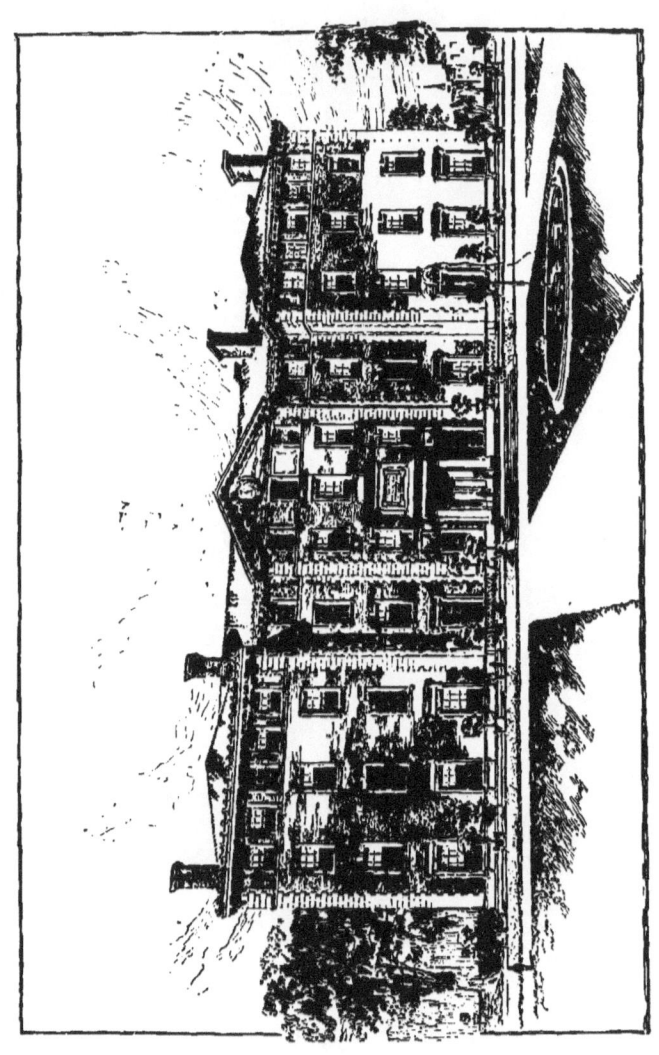

SCHERMERHORN HALL

MORNING EXERCISES

LAYING THE CORNER-STONE
OF THE
PHYSICS BUILDING
at 12 o'clock meridian

The Rev. MARVIN R. VINCENT, S.T.D.
> Officiating Chaplain

LAYING THE CORNER-STONE by OGDEN N. ROOD, A.M.
> Professor of Physics

ADDRESS by J. HOWARD VAN AMRINGE, LL.D.
> Dean of the College

LAYING THE CORNER-STONE
OF
SCHERMERHORN HALL
at 12:30 o'clock post meridian

The Rev. MORGAN DIX, S.T.D., D.C.L.
> Officiating Chaplain

LAYING THE CORNER-STONE by WILLIAM C. SCHERMERHORN, A.M.
> Chairman of the Trustees

ADDRESS by HENRY FAIRFIELD OSBORN, Sc.D.
> Da Costa Professor of Zoology

7

PHYSICS BUILDING

AFTERNOON EXERCISES

Music

Prayer by the Rev. Edward B. Coe, D.D.

Address by the President of the University

Presentation of National Colors on behalf of Lafayette Post, G. A. R., by Richard W. Meade, Rear Admiral, U. S. N. (Retired), Post-Commander

Music
"The Star-Spangled Banner," by the 71st Regiment Band

Acceptance of the Colors by the President

Singing of the Dedication Ode
Air, " Integer Vitæ "

Address by the Hon. Abram S. Hewitt, LL.D.

Music

Address by Charles W. Eliot, LL.D.
President of Harvard University

Benediction by the Rt. Rev. Henry C. Potter, D.D., LL.D.

Music

CARMEN DEDICATIONIS

CARMEN, O MATER, QVATIENTE MENTEM
CORDE ET IN MAGNO IVVENVM SENVMQVE
GAVDIO, CANTARE TIBI SONORVM
    POSCIMVR OMNES.

TE FREQVENS CINGIT IVVENVM CORONA,
OBVIA ET PORTIS HILARIS CATERVA,
HANC IN ÆTERNVM DECORAMVS ÆDEM
    CARMINE NOSTRO.

HIC NOVO LVCEBIS AMORE SEMPER
GLORIAM EXAVGENS STVDIO TVORVM,
HIC VIRVM CLARORVM ANIMO RECORDANS
    ALMA VIREBIS.

CRESCAT O SEMPER NOVA CRESCAT ÆTAS!
LÆTA SIC OMNIS FLVET HORA, MATER,
LÆTA IAM NATIS ET IN OMNE TEMPVS
    LÆTA FVTVRIS.

HARRY THURSTON PECK

10

GRAND MARSHAL

George G. DeWitt, '67

MARSHALS

Henry Dudley, '61

J. Visscher Wheeler, '65

Julien T. Davies, '66

John A. Church, '67

Nicholas Fish, '67

Henry D. Babcock, '68

F. dePeyster Foster, '68

William Allen Smith, '68

John C. F. Randolph, '69

Elwyn Waller, '70

Francis P. Kinnicutt, M.D., '71

Alexander B. Simonds, '73

Robert C. Cornell, '74

Eben E. Olcott, '74

B. Aymar Sands, '74

B. Bryson Delavan, M.D., '75

Edward L. Partridge, M.D., '75

Isaac N. Seligman, '76

Francis S. Bangs, '78

T. Matlack Cheesman, M.D., '78

Frank W. Jackson, M.D., '79

S. Victor Constant, '80

M. Allen Starr, M.D., '80

Reginald H. Sayre, M.D., '81

Howard Van Sinderen, '81

William T. Lawson, '82

William Barclay Parsons, '82

Edwin B. Holden, '83

Walter B. James, M.D., '83

George A. Suter, '83

W. Fellowes Morgan, '84

Samuel C. Van Dusen, '84

Grant Squires, '85

Edward P. Casey, '86

Edward DeWitt, '86

Charles N. Dowd, M.D., '86

William Jay Schieffelin, '87

Richard T. Wilson, Jr., '87

William K. Draper, M.D., '88

Edwin Gould, '88

D. LeRoy Dresser, '89

VanHorne Norrie, M.D., '89

Cortlandt Field Bishop, '91

Joseph Larocque, Jr., '92

STUDENT MARSHALS

EDWARD HAMILTON DALY, '96, *Senior Marshal in Charge.*

COLLEGE
SAMUEL S. SEWARD, JR., '96, *Senior Marshal.*

JOHN D. IRVING, '96   BURDETTE K. MARVIN, '97

WILLIAM B. GUNTON, '97   EUGENE E. SPIEGELBERG, '97

MORTON K. AVERILL, '98   GEORGE P. FORT, '99

FRANK H. CURRY, '98   ARTHUR A. FOWLER, '99

RALPH B. POMEROY, '98   THEOPHILUS PARSONS, '99

BARNARD COLLEGE
ELSIE W. CLEWS, '96, *Senior Marshal.*

AGNES BALDWIN, '97   ROSALIE BLOOMINGDALE, '98

LOUISE S. BROWNELL

SCHOOL OF LAW
HERMANN G. FRIEDMANN, '96, *Senior Marshal.*

WILLIAM C. WHITE, '96   FREDERIC WHITE SHEPARD, '97

HENRY A. UTERHART, '96   MONCURE MARCH, '97

ANSON McB. BEARD, '98   GROSVENOR HYDE BACKUS, '97

JAY L. THOMPSON, '98   GUSTAVUS T. KIRBY, '98

SCHOOL OF MEDICINE

JAMES W. MacNIDER, '96, *Senior Marshal.*

CHARLES E. BOYNTON, '96

CARLYLE E. SUTPHEN, JR., '96

THEODORUS BAILEY, '98

MARION WHITACRE, '99

WILLIAM W. VIBBERT, '98

EDWARD M. BROWN, '98

CLARENCE W. CAMPBELL, '98

WALTER A. BASTEDO, '99

SCHOOL OF MINES

WALTER A. SLICHTER, '96, *Senior Marshal.*

EDWARD D. TOMPKINS, '96

GEORGE T. MORSE, '96

ORLEANS LONGACRE, '98

ARTHUR WARE, '98

ALLEN F. EDWARDS, '98

CHARLES M. CLARK, '97

JOHN W. GOODRIDGE, '97

ALEXANDER S. FARMER, '97

ALFRED W. HARRISON, '99

FRANK S. DICKERSON, '99

HENRY C. CARPENTER, '99

SCHOOLS OF
POLITICAL SCIENCE, PHILOSOPHY, AND PURE SCIENCE

FREDERIC L. LUQUEER, *Senior Marshal.*

MILO R. MALTBIE

HERBERT M. JOHNSTONE

FRANK H. S. NOBLE

THE SITE OF KING'S COLLEGE

IN a letter to the Secretary of the Society for the Propagation of the Gospel in Foreign Parts, written in 1702, during the reign of Queen Anne, Governor Lewis Morris quaintly and prophetically observes :

"The Queen has a Farm of about 32 Acres of Land, wch Rents for £36 p. Ann : Tho the Church Wardens & Veſtry have petitioned for it & my Ld four months gave ym a promiſe of it the proceeding has been ſo ſlow that they begin to fear the Success wont anſwer the expectation. I believe her Maty. would readily grant it to the Society for the aſking. N. York is the Center of Engliſh America & a Proper Place for a Colledge,—& that Farm in a little time will be of conſiderable Value, & it's pity ſuch a thing ſhould be loſt for want of aſking, wch at another time wont be ſo Easily obtained."

Governor Morris's letter contains the earliest reference to the "Queen's" or "King's" Farm, as it was generally called, and also offers the first suggestion of founding a College in the Province of New York. Some fifty years elapsed before that event occurred. On October 31, 1754, a Charter was granted to "THE GOVERNORS OF THE COLLEGE OF THE PROVINCE OF NEW YORK IN THE CITY OF NEW YORK IN AMERICA." Trinity Church having in the interval acquired title to the King's Farm, the Rector and Church Wardens forthwith delivered to the Governors a lease and release of that portion of the Farm lying on the West side of Broad-

KING'S COLLEGE

REPRODUCED, THROUGH THE COURTESY OF MR. WILLIAM LORING ANDREWS, FROM A PRINT PUBLISHED IN THE NEW YORK MAGAZINE IN 1790, SHOWING THE BUILDING BEFORE ALTERATIONS WERE MADE, AND AFTER THE REMOVAL OF THE CROWN WHICH ORIGINALLY SURMOUNTED THE CUPOLA.

way, between Barclay and Murray Streets, and extending down to the Hudson River, described as being "in the skirts of the City." Steps were at once taken to procure plans for suitable buildings, and to raise money with which to erect them ; liberal contributions were received, and on August 23, 1756, the corner-stone of King's College was laid by Sir Charles Hardy, then Governor of the Province. The stone, which has fortunately been preserved, bears the following inscription :

"HVJVS COLLEGII, REGALIS DICTI, REGIO DIPLOMATE CONSTITVTI
IN HONOREM DEI O.M. ATQ; IN ECCLESIÆ REIQ; PVBLICÆ
EMOLVMENTVM, PRIMVM HVNC LAPIDEM POSVIT VIR PRÆCEL
LENTISSIMVS, CAROLVS HARDY, EQVES AVRATVS, HVJVS PROVINCIÆ
PRÆFECTVS DIGNISSIMVS. AVGTI. DIE 23°, AN. DOM. MDCCLVI."

In 1760 the fact is noted in the records that "The College buildings were so far completed that the officers and students began to lodge and mess therein." In honor of George II., and in accordance with the terms of the Charter, the building thus completed was designated "King's College," and the original crown which surmounted it remains, a witness to its royal foundation. The Rev. Dr. Burnaby, an English traveller, writes: "The College when finished will be exceedingly handsome. It is to be built on three sides of a quadrangle fronting Hudson's or North River, and will be the most beautifully situated of any College, I believe, in the world"; and President Myles Cooper describes the College as it existed in 1773, as distant about a hundred and fifty yards "from the Hudson River, which it overlooks, commanding from the eminence on which it stands a most extensive and beautiful prospect."

In April, 1776, upon the request of the Committee of Safety, the College was prepared for the reception of troops, the students were dispersed ; and the library and apparatus were removed to the City Hall. During the Revolution the buildings were used both by the American and British troops as barracks and for hospital purposes.

The College exercises, suspended during the pendency of hostilities, were resumed in 1784. On May 1, 1784, an Act was passed by the Legislature of the State of New York, entitled "AN ACT FOR GRANTING CERTAIN PRIVILEGS TO THE COLLEGE HERETOFORE CALLED KING'S COLLEGE, FOR ALTERING THE NAME AND CHARTER THEREOF, AND ERECTING AN UNIVERSITY WITHIN THE STATE." Under this Act the College received the name "COLUMBIA"—"a word and name then for the first time recognized anywhere in law and history"; and the administration of the College passed to the Regents of the University.

.Three years later the management of the College was transferred to "The Trustees of Columbia College in the City of New York," as the corporation has ever since been known. On the occasion of the first Commencement of the College under its new name, held April 10, 1787, the Legislature, upon the motion of Alexander Hamilton, adjourned in order that its members might attend, and in 1789 the Commencement was honored by the presence of President Washington and all the principal officers of the Government of the United States. After the Revolution an effort was made to restore the buildings to a condition suitable for educational purposes; but the result was not fully accomplished until 1820, when two wings were added, greatly increasing the capacity and convenience of the buildings. A chapel and library were also built, and in 1829 a building for a Grammar School was erected adjacent to the College. President Moore, in his memorial address, presents a pleasing picture of "the stately sycamores on the Green, the old buildings, the great staircase, the Chapel, with its strange hanging gallery." And Mr. Jay, in his Centennial address, tells us that these venerable trees had an historic interest, from the fact, which as a boy he heard from the lips of Judge Benson, that they were carried to the Green and planted by the Judge himself, and by Chief Justice Jay, Chancellor Livingston, and Recorder Harrison.

COLUMBIA COLLEGE IN 1828

REPRODUCED FROM A PRINT PUBLISHED IN THE NEW YORK MIRROR

A member of the Class of '39 gives the following description of the College as it appeared in his day, when it "occupied a plot of ground bounded by Church Street, Murray Street and College Place. The building was of brick, covered with stucco, painted light brown, with trimmings of free stone. The front was to the south. At the east and west ends, respectively, were two houses occupied by members of the faculty, which projected considerably beyond the middle buildings; all were three stories high, and there was an old-fashioned belfry in the middle; it was a picturesque old structure, unmistakably academic. In front was a Green of considerable size, bordered by large sycamores. The place had an air of conventional quiet and seclusion, and was delightful in Summer when the shadows of the broad leaves rested on the light brown walls and the flagstones of the walk. The middle of the edifice was devoted to the Chapel and Library. The latter occupied the second floor, and on the floor below were the lecture rooms. The location was about the center of the fashionable part of the city."

For many years the College Green preserved its verdure and tranquillity in the midst of encroaching commerce, but by degrees it was intersected with streets. "Chapel Street" and "College Place" for a time marked the site, but even these have now disappeared. In 1854 the Trustees determined upon removal, but the exercises were continued until May 7, 1857, when the last service was held in the old Chapel, the ancient corner-stone was disinterred from its long resting place to be borne to its new home, and the halls which had echoed to the march of history were abandoned forever.

THE PRESENT SITE

THE Botanical Garden, between Fifth and Sixth Avenues, Forty-ninth and Fiftieth Streets, was selected as the site to which the College should be removed from Murray Street, and Mr. Upjohn was employed to prepare a design for the new buildings. The execution of this project, however, was found to be impracticable, for the time being, on account of the expense involved; and in November, 1856, the Trustees purchased of the Institution for the Instruction of the Deaf and Dumb twenty lots situated on Madison Avenue, between Forty-ninth and Fiftieth Streets. The purchase was made upon favorable terms, and the action of the Trustees was influenced largely by the fact that the buildings of the Institution were available for the immediate use of the College, with but slight alterations. The opening services were held in the Chapel of the "New College," as it was called, May 12, 1857. The buildings consisted of a large edifice of brick and brown stucco, standing on the high ground near Fiftieth Street, with adjacent buildings at either end, one of which served as a Chapel, and the other as a residence for professors. President King and his family at first occupied rooms in the main building, which also furnished a number of class and lecture rooms. The principal architectural feature of the central building was a lofty portico; and the group of buildings, shaded by a row of fine old trees on a beautiful lawn sloping southward, presented a pleasing and dignified appearance. "The present location of the College" is described in the

COLUMBIA COLLEGE IN 1860

REPRODUCED FROM A PRINT PUBLISHED IN APPLETON'S MAGAZINE

Evening Post of May 11, 1857, as "a delightful one, and undesirable only on account of the distance up town. . . . The site is on a commanding eminence, affording an extensive and pleasant view."

Subsequently, the Trustees purchased the lots comprising the remainder of the block, including a factory, which was afterwards used for the School of Mines. The buildings continued to be occupied with but little change until 1860, when the President's House was erected. In 1876 the West wing was removed. In 1877–78 the present North wing of the School of Mines Building was erected ; and in 1881–82 the Library and Law School and Hamilton Hall were built. The original building was torn down in 1892 ; and in 1897 the University will be removed to its new and far more spacious site on Morningside Heights.

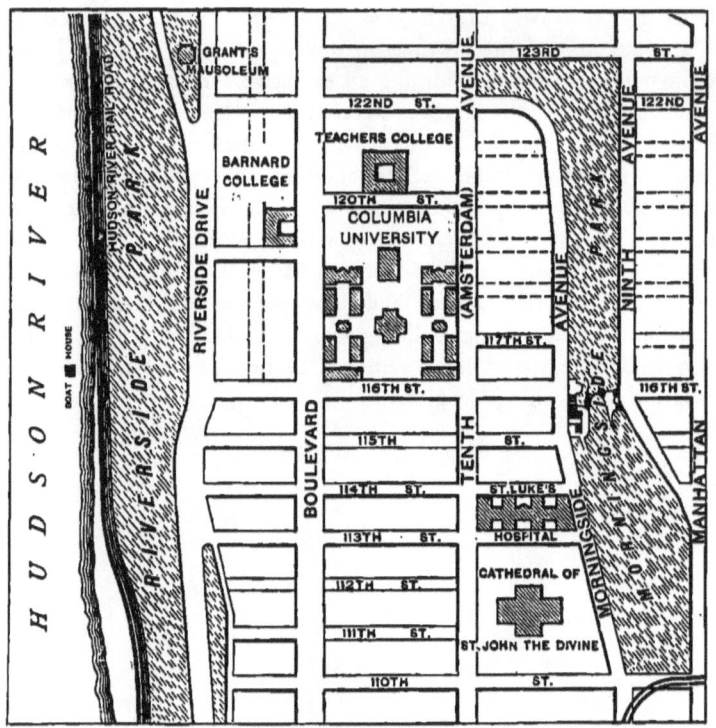

MAP OF MORNINGSIDE HEIGHTS

THE NEW SITE

T HE history of the new site dates from 1701, when Jacob deKey purchased his farm from the City; but it was not until September 16, 1776, that the event occurred which renders it memorable, and which can best be described in the words of an eye-witness:

"On Monday morning, about ten o'Clock, a party of the Enemy confifting of Highlanders, Heffians, the Light Infantry, Grenadiers, and Englifh Troops, (Number uncertain), attack'd our advanc'd Party, commanded by Coll. Knowlton at Martje Davits Fly. They were oppofed with fpirit, and foon made to retreat to a clear Field, fouthweft of that about two hundred paces, where they lodged themfelves behind a Fence covered with Bufhes our People attack'd them in Turn, and caufed them to retreat a fecond Time, leaving five dead on the Spot, we purfued them to a Buckwheat Field on the Top of a high Hill, diftance about four hundred paces, where they received a confiderable Reinforcement, with feveral Field Pieces, and there made a Stand a very brifk Action enfued at this Place, which continued about Two Hours our People at length worfted them a third Time, caufed them to fall back into an Orchard, from thence acrofs a Hollow, and up another Hill not far diftant from their own Lines . . ."

So wrote General Clinton to the New York Convention describing the Battle of Harlem, which had been fought two days previously, on September 16, 1776. He presents a vivid picture, and we need but follow his description, beginning at "Martje Davits Fly," the meadow lying in the valley between One Hundred and Twenty-fifth and One Hundred and Twenty-ninth Streets, near Amsterdam Avenue, across the level ground to the foot of the northerly slope of Morningside Park, and up the hillside to the "Buckwheat Field on the Top of a high Hill," and we find ourselves upon the field where the battle was fought: the field where Columbia is to stand. What was once the buckwheat field, made memorable by the first battle in which the American troops faced the British and routed them, has become the new site of Columbia; and, where Colonel Knowlton fell the walls of the University are now rising.

The College which the traveller of a hundred years ago described as the most beautifully situated in the world once more looks forth upon the waters of the Hudson, but from a higher vantage ground and with the broader vision of the University. To the natural beauty of the situation, which fits it so pre-eminently to be the home of learning, is added the element of historic interest, associating the University of to-day still more inseparably with the College of the Revolution.

THE NEW BUILDINGS

THE land upon which the buildings are to be erected comprises a little more than seventeen acres. It is divided naturally into two levels. The southerly level, or plateau, which is one hundred and fifty feet above high water and includes about ten acres, is the higher, and varies in elevation from five to ten feet above the surrounding streets. The buildings in process of erection are being constructed chiefly upon the higher plateau, thus preserving a fine grove of oaks and chestnuts that adorns the northern portion of the grounds, and leaving space for future development. The buildings are arranged in a series of quadrangles, but with spacious openings on the streets and avenues. The Library, already partially built, is to form the centre of the group, and its proportions and design will render it one of the most commanding features of Morningside Heights. The main approach to the grounds is from One Hundred and Sixteenth Street, by a broad flight of steps and a court 375 feet in width by 200 feet in depth. Another flight of steps will lead to the portico of the Library.

Purely classic in style, the Library resembles in form a Greek cross, and will be surmounted by a dome. The width of the building will be 192 feet, and the height of the dome 135 feet. It will be constructed of Indiana limestone on a basement of Milford granite. The main floor will be devoted to administration and to several reading rooms. The general reading room will occupy the centre of the

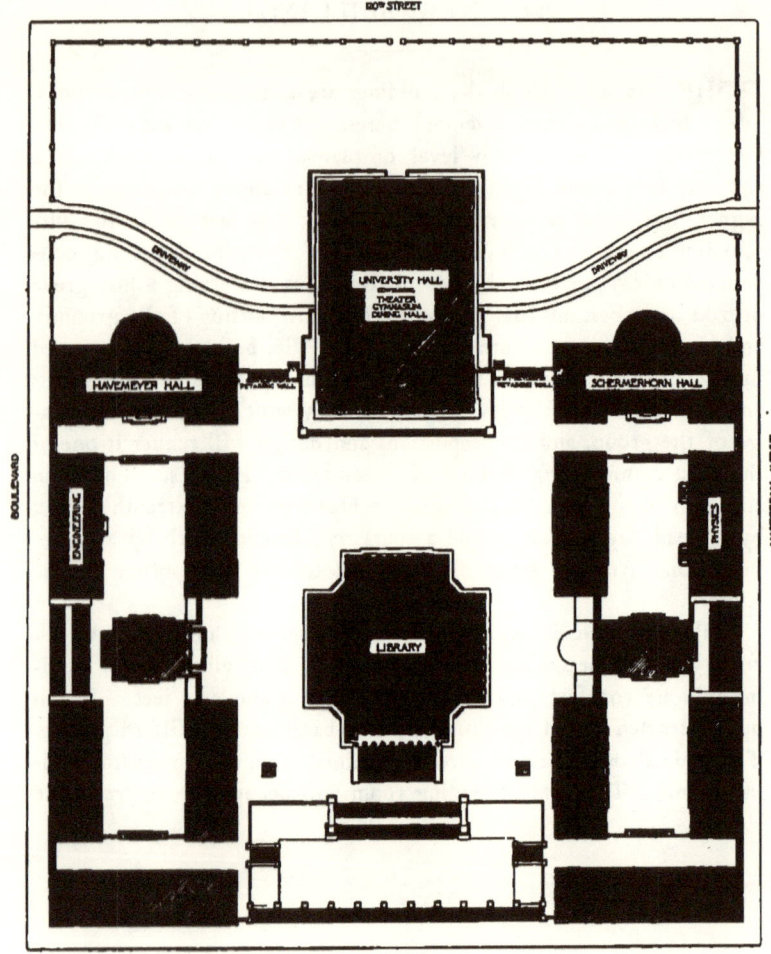

PLAN OF THE NEW BUILDINGS AND GROUNDS

building under the dome, and will be nearly square in form, 80 feet in width, with a seating capacity for two hundred and twenty-five readers. The Avery Architectural Library, the Law Library, and other collections will be placed in the wings. The estimated capacity of the building is more than one million volumes. The Building is a memorial of Abiel Abbot Low, and is given by his son, Seth Low, the President of the University.

To the East and West of the Library are to be the Chapel and the Assembly Hall, the latter being intended as a place of meeting for student organizations, such as the Literary and Debating Societies and the Glee Club, and for public lectures; and generally to serve as a centre for the social life of the students. Opposite each of these buildings will be an entrance from the adjoining avenue.

Schermerhorn Hall, the northeasterly building on the plan, is the gift of Mr. William C. Schermerhorn, the Chairman of the Trustees, and will be devoted to the Natural Sciences. It will contain the museums, laboratories, lecture rooms and seminars of the departments of Botany, Geology, Mineralogy, and the DaCosta Department of Zoology. The adjoining building, designated as the " Physics Building " only until the name of a donor may be substituted, will contain in the first instance the departments of Physics, Mechanics, Astronomy, and Mathematics, or, perhaps, Modern Languages. Ultimately it is expected that the entire building will be used by the Department of Physics. These buildings are also under construction. They are to be built of the over-burned brick of a dull-red color, generally known as Harvard brick, and of Indiana limestone. In style they are in keeping with the Library, and represent to some extent a reversion to the best construction of the Colonial period. Schermerhorn Hall offers a pleasing reminder of old King's College. Their simple and dignified lines and generous windows fitly express the purpose for which they are to be used, and the intention of the design to subserve the needs of modern scientific education.

29

Havemeyer Hall, which is to occupy the northwesterly angle of the upper plateau, will be erected as a memorial of Frederick C. Havemeyer, by his sons, Henry O., Frederick C., Theodore A., and Thomas J. Havemeyer; his daughters Kate B. Belloni and S. Louisa Jackson, and his nephew Charles H. Senff. It has been especially planned for the study of Chemistry, and eventually will be devoted exclusively to that department, but temporarily the upper floor will be used by the students in Architecture.

Plans have also been prepared for the adjoining Engineering Building, as well as for the University Building, and these also will soon be in course of construction. The University Building will be situated immediately to the north of the Library, about 200 feet distant, and, next to the Library, will be the most important and conspicuous building on the grounds. The southerly portion of the building facing the Library quadrangle is designed as a Memorial Hall, which it is hoped may be the gift of the Alumni, to serve both as a monument of distinguished graduates and as a dining-hall for the officers, students, and alumni of the university. Connecting with the Hall and on the same level is the University Theatre, having a seating capacity of 2,500. Under the Theatre is the Gymnasium, and under Memorial Hall the engine room and power plant. The building has a frontage of 180 feet, and a depth of 240 feet. It is situated on the dividing line between the upper and lower levels, and the difference in grade renders it possible to adapt the building to its various uses most advantageously. It will be rendered easily accessible by a carriage road intersecting the grounds at One Hundred and Nineteenth Street, and passing through the building. For Commencements and other public occasions, the theatre, the dining hall, and other communicating rooms of the southerly portion of the building, may be used together, and will provide spacious and beautiful accommodations.

Of the other buildings indicated on the plan, the particular use

HAVEMEYER HALL

remains to be determined by the rapidly increasing needs of the University. That they will be provided when required there can be little doubt.

The buildings now upon the grounds are West Hall, on the Boulevard near One Hundred and Eighteenth Street, which will be used as a dormitory for instructors and university students until the land which it occupies is required for a lecture hall ; and South Hall, at the corner of Amsterdam Avenue and One Hundred and Sixteenth Street, which will serve temporarily for the College. It is hoped that this may soon give place to a more spacious and suitable building in which the College shall find a permanent home.

To realize to the full the great opportunities afforded by its environment is the duty that now confronts the University. The loftier elevation and greater extent of its new site should find expression in the higher ideals and broader scholarship of the University, in an influence for good more far-reaching and potent. That these results will follow is best assured by the progress that the University has made during the past few years under conditions far less favorable. To the advancement of the highest, and broadest, and soundest learning the University stands pledged, irrevocably; while upon the material side the best professional talent, after the most careful study, has projected the lines of future development. The generosity of Columbia's graduates, officers and friends has already afforded conspicuous evidence both of their confidence in the work that the University is doing and of their belief in the complete success of her present enterprise. And we may look forward with confidence to the complete realization of the ideal presented by George William Curtis when the purchase of the site was in contemplation :

"This is the moment to secure this crowning opportunity for the old college to become the magnificent and adequate representative of the just aspirations of the city for an institution which is symbolical of the higher interests of every great and prosperous com-

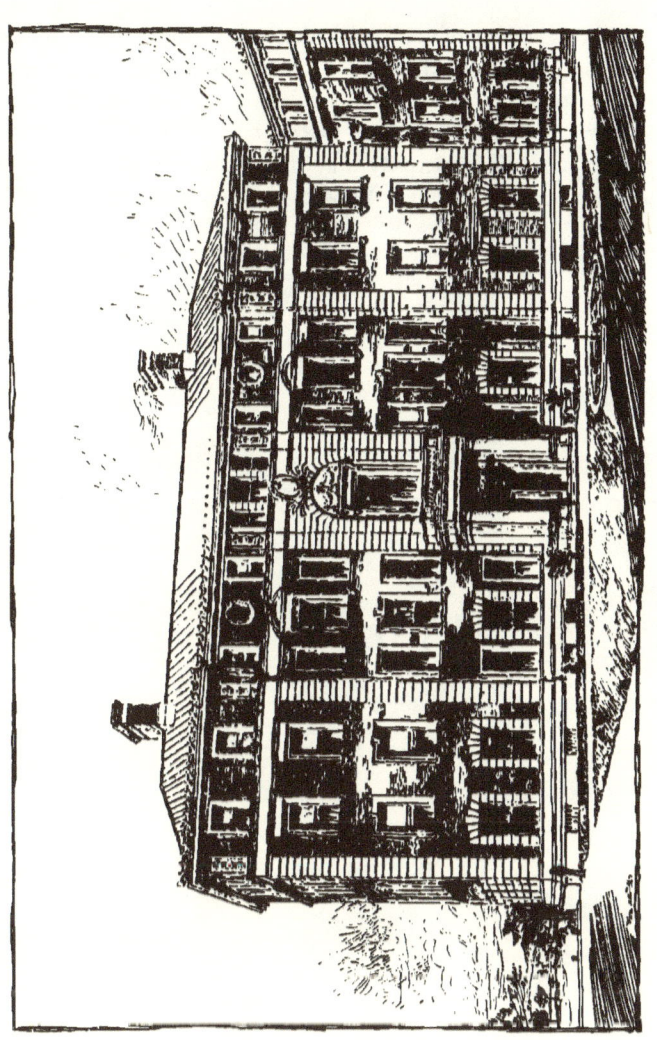

ENGINEERING BUILDING

. munity.   For the abounding wealth that every year accumulates here, what finer disposition could there be than generous gifts for Columbia ? Athens has no loftier names of places than the Garden, the Porch, the Academy.   What they were to the city of the violet crown, a prompt and splendid generosity may make the college of the great Revolutionary patriots of New York to the city of their children."

IN LUMINE TUO
VIDEBIMUS
LUMEN

PROCEEDINGS AND ADDRESSES

THE corner-stones of Schermerhorn Hall and the Physics Building were laid, and the Dedication of the New Site took place
on Saturday, the second of May, in the presence of the Governor of
the State of New York, the Mayor of the City of New York, the
Trustees and Faculties of the University, representatives of other universities and other distinguished guests, and an assemblage of about
five thousand people. The National Colors were presented by Rear
Admiral Meade, on behalf of Lafayette Post, and accepted by the
President of the University, and addresses were made by the speakers
named in the programme.

The following telegram was received from the President of the
United States :

Executive Mansion,
Washington, D. C.,
May 2nd, 1896.

Hon. Seth Low,
       President of Columbia College.

As a lover of New York, interested in all that is related to her advancement and
prestige, I congratulate her citizens and those having the affairs of Columbia College in
their keeping on the event of to-day and all it foretells of the increased importance and
usefulness of the ancient and fondly cherished institution of learning whose new location
is appropriately dedicated by her devoted sons and those who appreciate what she has so
long and so well done for higher education.

Grover Cleveland.

ADDRESS

By J. Howard Van Amringe, LL.D.

DEAN OF THE COLLEGE

———

Mr. President, Gentlemen of the Trustees and Faculties, and
Fellow Alumni:

ONE hundred and forty years ago, the first stone of the first building for this College was laid by Sir Charles Hardy, Governor-
General of the Province of New York. The entire teaching force of
the institution then consisted of Dr. Johnson, the President, and Mr.
Leonard Cutting, a tutor, and the total number of matriculated students was fifteen.

In the year following this ceremony was created the first professorship, that of "Mathematics and Natural History," under which
title was included a wide range of scientific subjects—and yet not so
wide but that the incumbent was charged also with instruction in the
Greek and Latin languages.

This professorship seems to have grown and multiplied, as some
forms of zoöphytes do, by gemmules, which drop off, complete and
living entities that reproduce themselves indefinitely in like manner.
From it has sprung a good part of all the scientific activities that now
distinguish the College. And it is a felicitous circumstance, that the
first of the buildings for strictly instructional purposes to be dedicated
upon this noble site of the new Columbia, should be one for departments which are the legitimate and necessary issue of the first professorship in the old Columbia, out of which has been developed, *per*

varios casus, et tot discrimina rerum, this University in all it its present dignity and future promise.

I deem it not without significance that the educational buildings of which the corner-stones are laid this morning should be those devoted to science in some of its most interesting and important aspects. This priority of dedication, to whatever consideration it may be due, exemplifies, in a marked manner, the vast change that has been wrought, within a comparatively recent period, in the opinions of men as to the importance and the influence of exact scientific research.

It is not very long ago, just seventy-one years next Monday, the 4th of May, that a scholar of repute in his day, a son of Columbia and for nearly half a century one of its Trustees, in an address to his fellow alumni, warned them against certain forms of refined scientific pursuit as a "frivolity of education." The "frivolity" to which he referred—the classification of "the stripes of tulips, the colors of butterflies and other things of a still more unsubstantial nature"—diversified and sedulously followed, enabled the great Darwin and his coadjutors to reconstruct the realm of ideas and, by giving a truer meaning, add rarer charm to the animate and inanimate world about us; and provision for this "frivolity," and others of like kind, is now a vital part of the plan of development of this University.

It is well within the memory of very many, perhaps the most, of us here that the prosecution of science was, in general, regarded with apprehension, as inimical to reverence and faith. Such fear has passed away; it is no longer, at least, a prevalent and restrictive force. The advance of scientific discovery in many directions, the better co-ordination of the various kinds of knowledge, the clearer perception of limitations of inquiry, a more accurate discrimination between what is undoubted fact and what is disputable interpretation and inference, the more philosophic disposition of investigators in different fields to put themselves each in the other's place, and the increasing prevalence of catholicity of spirit, have, in the intelligent community, begotten keen expectancy in place of apprehensiveness, eagerness for the extension of accurate knowledge without fear of result as to cherished beliefs.

It was but the other day that Rontgen, the physicist, noticed a few lines and discolorations on a paper that lay upon a table in his laboratory. These apparently trivial objects excited his trained scientific attention, aroused in him the "divine curiosity" of which Plato spoke and which is the impelling force in all intellectual advancement —and hence the discovery that has lately electrified the world. Nowhere is there any feeling but one of delight and wonder at this discovery. There is no thought, certainly no suggestion, as there would, doubtless, not long since, have been, that, in these marvellous X-rays, which pierce through the solid flesh, light up the secret and dark places of the animal frame and almost lay bare the human heart, there is anything even remotely dangerous to that faith which is the life of the soul.

Indeed, the verities of the case seem to warrant a further and more pronounced statement. Not only has the stream of public feeling in this regard ceased to flow in channels of doubt, apprehension and reproof, it has changed its bed and become

" The current that with gentle murmur glides "

in courses of hope and encouragement. Scientific investigation that once, in its insufficiency and arrogance, was thought by many, and not, perhaps, without reason, to encourage materialism, the limiting of man's vision, intellectual and spiritual, to the narrow confines of this little world, is, in its fuller and more diversified activity and more reverent prosecution, seen to foster a high idealism, to be, in fact, a potent instrument in the cultivation of a rational humility, of a necessary faith in things beyond the senses, of a truer appreciation of men's place in nature and of his spiritual obligations. Scientific research, by the innumerable and incalculable benefits which through it have been conferred upon the world—in bringing into closer relationship and easier communion the scattered peoples of the globe; in ameliorating the lot of all sorts and conditions of men; in illustrating and enforcing the Divine precept as to the essential brotherhood of man; in prolonging human life and in enriching it in every way; in inciting a spirit of intelligent inquiry into all questions that nature, or man in his various relations, presents, and in providing methods of examination and presentment, careful, acute, exhaustive, logical, that have modified, and even revolutionized, those once prevalent in many departments of learning—has revealed itself as a trustworthy and valuable ally of all the better influences, of whatever sort, that tend to the elevation of mankind, in spiritual no less than in material things, to the advancement of truth as it affects the soul not less than as it concerns the body.

Truth is truth, wherever and howsoever it may be found; and every well-established truth is an aid, and not a hindrance, to the ascertainment and more perfect interpretation of any other and of all truth. To the discovery, elucidation, promulgation and enforcement of truth, in science, letters and life, this fair site and all the buildings that may hereafter adorn it are to be this day solemnly consecrated. "As for the truth, it endureth and is always strong; it liveth and conquereth for evermore. With her there is no acceptance of persons or rewards. . . . Neither in her judgment is any unrighteousness; and she is the strength, kingdom, power and majesty, of all ages."

Copies of the Royal Charter and of the Charters granted by the State.

The Statutes of the University and the By-Laws of the Trustees.

The President's last annual report of the University.

The last annual Catalogue of the University.

University Bulletin.

The General Catalogue of Officers and Alumni.

Description and views of the buildings.

The programme of the day's proceedings.

Newspapers of the day, and coins

WILLIAM C. SCHERMERHORN, A.M.

ADDRESS

By Henry Fairfield Osborn, Sc.D.

DA COSTA PROFESSOR OF ZÖLOGY

THE CORNER-STONES OF LEARNING

PASSING as we are to-day from one to another of these foundations of Literature, Philosophy and History, Chemical and Physical Science, who would not be stirred with the enthusiasm of learning? What naturalist, near or far, will not rejoice in the laying of the corner-stone of this Hall which we now dedicate to the studies beloved by Aristotle and Goethe, by Linnæus, Buffon and Lamarck, by Lyell, Darwin and Huxley, by Agassiz, Torrey and Dana?

The influence of these masters is bounded neither by time nor language. The close touch with nature which they have inspired makes the whole world kin. The incessant production and interchange of new truths tie together the naturalists of every country. Our political and social systems may reverse those of Russia, but such differences do not separate American and Russian naturalists. The history of the earth, the origin of its plants and animals, the secret hidden in the simple cell of the amoeba, or in the countless cells of the human brain, are the same in distant Siberia as upon this island. A new law discovered in these laboratories will not be estimated at our own valuation, for it will be neither new nor true here unless it is so everywhere. We may well say:

Mare sejuncta, veritate conjuncta

43

when we dedicate this building, and we may feel assured, in the generous emulation of scientific progress, that the benefits of Schermerhorn Hall will extend far beyond our shores if we set the example of broad research and build our instruction upon a scale worthy of this noble building.

A hundred thoughts of the past and future crowd upon us, but few can be expressed when an university is rising, like Minerva, in a single day. We would speak of the past, of the naturalists whose names are associated especially with this city, of Audubon, of Torrey or of Newberry. But these rising walls point to the future and prompt us to consider what will insure the true greatness of this and of its sister buildings. How shall we plan our research and instruction to produce the best results? What have we accomplished; what have we yet to do and how shall it be done? What are the especial needs of American scientific education to-day?

In the last quarter-century we have found much inspiration in Germany, but we can observe with satisfaction that England and France are now adopting certain features of our graduate schools. In continuing to study the best foreign models we are not sacrificing our independence; we are entering into the world spirit, which is the true spirit of science; we are endeavoring to put a right estimate upon our own position. We must build the best; we must join the learned circle of the universities of history—of Paris, of Bologna or of Cambridge; not in mere rivalry, but in the spirit of veneration for these institutions, in the love of science for its own sake. We look forward to the day when foreign students will come to America as we now go abroad. It is a great achievement that in taking so much from others we have maintained our individuality. Our essential advance is this: we have established the principle that in the college the student is learning, he is gathering in knowledge; in the university he is more than a learner. In school and college he is a consumer; in the university he must be both consumer and producer, and the criterion of our universities, of American scientists at large, is the extent and quality of their productiveness.

During this advance we have been under four great educational leaders: McCosh, Eliot, Gilman and Low, who have been keenly observant of this principle of production. Our debt to them and to the faculties associated with them can hardly be estimated. The elevation of these five buildings is but a mile-stone in the course of the most rapid university development ever seen in any country. Justly confident as we are in this progress, it would be over-confidence to suppose that we have as yet reached the general level of either Germany, France, or England. In three or four branches of science, perhaps, where our circumstances are especially favorable, we have struck the highest note, but certainly not in all. Moreover, if we candidly apply the criterion of productiveness not as to quantity, but as to quality, are we assured that our intellectual output is keeping pace with the material equipment of our universities? Are we now training natural philosophers of the calibre of Franklin, of Henry, or of Dana? The problem of the last twenty years has been to establish universities. We have established them. The problem of the next twenty years is to train thinkers of the highest type.

When we consider that the number of students has increased ten-fold, and that our educational facilities have multiplied a hundredfold, do we find a corresponding ratio in the increase of original thought? If not, and it is at least an open question, which is at fault, the American student or his educational environment? Our students are of the most virile Anglo-Saxon, Teutonic and Latin stock, and the stability of mental type is so assured that if there is a defect it must be in our methods of education. The very rapidity and eagerness so characteristic of our country and of our university growth are at once a sign of strength and a source of danger. The momentum of thought is not the momentum of a comet. In Amer-

ican social and political life there is the widespread impression that progress is represented by the mass multiplied by the rate, and the equally wide illusion as to the cardinal distinction between the consumption and the production of ideas. Nowhere, perhaps, is the confusion more prevalent than in this very city, which in its present state of civilization, is a great consumer and a comparatively limited producer of art, music, literature or science. This confusion to a certain extent permeates our scientific life and the government of even our best institutions, as shown by the annual exploitation of student numbers and by the timid attitude toward the standard of the higher degrees, as if mass and rate, rather than quality were our aim. We still have something to learn from the old world, and much from the past in our own country.

If this building, rising so rapidly that a year hence we expect to see here the full tide of work and thought, is to accomplish its purpose and become a centre of production in geology and biology, then we must plan to establish that type of educational environment which, within or without the walls of universities, in the experience of centuries, has nurtured thinkers of the highest rank. Figuratively speaking, there are four factors in such an environment, which we may term breadth, height, energy and repose.

Breadth, partly inborn and partly the result of training, is that sympathy with many sides of Nature which arises through widely extended observation, where many facts of many kinds are correlated. Every master like Helmholtz has become master of more than one science. It comes as a rare birthright, through the irresistible bias towards breadth characterizing a genius like Darwin, who unaided and unconsciously sought it in his self-education. But because it is rare we must supply the lack by insisting upon it in our scheme of instruction. In Chemistry and Physics, perhaps, it can be cultivated in the laboratory. The out-of-door sciences demand prolonged work in the field or upon the sea as well as in the laboratory.

Think what the world owes to the long voyages of Humboldt, of Darwin and of Dana.

The second factor, height, we recognize at once in specialization. The height we are seeking is specialization pursued with a continually widening horizon, as distinct from specialization with a continually narrowing horizon, and this also is gained only by prolonged and deep study of more than one subject.

Energy is the chief American characteristic in Science, as in other pursuits. It places us among the leaders in arctic, in geological and palæontological exploration, and in astronomical expeditions. These are among its more fortunate results, but, on the other hand, this very characteristic impels our students to superficiality, leading them to pursue six courses where they should only pursue three. It impels our professors to overload themselves with duties of administration and of practical affairs, as well as of teaching and research. In a manner it explains the unselfish willingness to work early and late and sacrifice everything to the duties of instruction, the over-teaching which burdens so many able men in our best institutions and finally cripples them. Our energy is of such disproportionate development that it is becoming a bar to research. In this country the children of science—the telegraph, steam and electrical transportation, the press—have become the greatest enemy of pure science, for they have produced a social and material environment utterly without repose, in which the most·coveted thing is a wholly undisturbed hour. If this be true, and every close observer of our scientific life must admit it, our greatest need is that repose which affords time for reflection, time for thought, when, after long inductive observation, there comes the sudden illumination of a discovery.

Without repose even genius will not liquefy the gases, will not discover Argon or Helium, will not send rays of light through solid objects, will not find the unknown factor in evolution, will not disclose the relations of the chromatin and archoplasm in the cell. An

47

eminent English biologist recently spoke of Darwin's invalidism, contracted during the "Beagle" voyage, as a blessing in disguise. During forty years it caused him suffering, but it also insured him the prolonged days, weeks, and years of undisturbed thought which has revolutionized the thought of the world. We need not go beyond the walls of this university for an illustration. You remember that Röntgen announced his discovery of the X-rays with the law that, unlike light rays, they were *not* reflected. Physicists everywhere began experiments with feverish energy. You know how reporters and magazine editors besieged every physicist whose door was not doubly barred. . One of our own colleagues, however, succeeded in resisting invasion for some weeks. At the end of a period of self-imprisonment came the simple announcement from Professor Rood, "I have discovered that the X-rays *are* reflected." In this discovery lies the chief addition to our knowledge of the physical properties of the Röntgen rays.

Repose is the feature of the student's ideal environment which our scientific forefathers enjoyed. It is an absolute requisite from boyhood upwards if we are to rear men of a high order of originality in the production of new ideas.

In the rapid rise of our educational institutions we have added breadth, yet there is room for far more. We have added specialization and energy : we have, if anything, diminished the opportunities for quiet undisturbed work. Upon those who are governing it must be impressed : give your best teachers time, and ample means to live. Fewer teachers, fewer students and fewer subjects, if need be, where the resources are limited. Let no original thinker feel the *res angusta domi* and destroy his finest powers in the struggle for subsistence. Upon our teachers it must be impressed : do not multiply subjects ; give your students, young and old, time to think ; make provision for deliberate thought throughout the whole scale of education, beginning in the home and school.

Let us therefore in this building establish the corner-stones of learning—breadth, standing for thoroughness of preparation and wideness of horizon; height, for specialization; energy, for determination in the prosecution of research; and repose, for undisturbed observation and induction. It is the symmetrical and balanced cultivation of all these factors which will make Schermerhorn Hall a birthplace of discoveries, a permanent monument to its generous founder, worthy of Columbia University, and a new force in American science.

ARTICLES PLACED IN THE CORNER-STONE

Copies of the Royal Charter and of the Charters granted by the State.

The Statutes of the University and the By-Laws of the Trustees.

A copy of Mr. Schermerhorn's letter of gift, and of the Trustees' resolutions accepting the same and designating the building "Schermerhorn Hall."

The President's last annual report of the University.

The last annual Catalogue of the University.

University Bulletin.

The General Catalogue of Officers and Alumni.

Description and views of the buildings.

The programme of the day's proceedings.

Newspapers of the day and coins.

SETH LOW, LL.D.
PRESIDENT OF THE UNIVERSITY

ADDRESS

By Seth Low, LL.D.,
PRESIDENT OF THE UNIVERSITY

Gentlemen of the Trustees; Professors, Alumni and Students
of Columbia University; Ladies and Gentlemen, our
Friends and Guests:

WE are met to-day to dedicate to a new use this historic ground.
Already it is twice consecrated. In the Revolutionary War
this soil drank the blood of patriots, willingly shed for the independence of the land. Since then, for three generations, it has witnessed
the union of science and of brotherly kindness devoted to the care of
humanity suffering from the most mysterious of all the ills that flesh
is heir to. To-day we dedicate it in the same spirit of loyalty to the
country and of devotion to mankind to the inspiring uses of a venerable and historic university.

How characteristic all this is of the city of New York. As
early as 1686 Gov. Dongan, in his charter, spoke of the city as a
"historic city." And indeed it is. Here was inaugurated the government of the United States under which we live, where Washington was sworn in as the first President of the new nation by Robert
R. Livingston, a son of Columbia College. But how hard it is to
preserve the sense of historic value in the midst of conditions that
are undergoing perpetual change! This is not even the first removal
of Columbia College from its original site close by the City Hall.
And yet we have courage to-day to hope that the university here will

enter upon its permanent home. If this site were upon the ordinary grade of the city we should be no more secure here than we have been elsewhere. But upon this noble eminence, flanked to the east and west by parks and precipices, it would seem that we can continue to abide without fear of disturbance, at least until the navigation of the air supersedes the roadways of the solid earth and until, for that reason, business chooses the lofty places of the earth because of their accessibility in preference to the plains. In the meanwhile it is not to be forgotten that the life that is to inhabit the buildings that are rising here, the life that is to animate teacher and scholar, student and investigator alike, is the same full, rich life that has been gathering power to serve and power to inspire, from generation to generation, during all the eventful years since it had its origin as King's College in the small city of New York in 1754. The things that are seen change and pass away ; but the things that are not seen endure.

It would be hard, I think, to find a situation more ideally suited to be the home of this university. Here Columbia will once again look out upon the waters of the Hudson as King's College looked out upon them so many years ago. And as she looks how can she fail to realize at once the vast continent behind her that she is set to serve, and the salt sea beyond her that washes the shores of many nations and reminds her that God has made of one blood all the peoples of the earth. Both the water and the land upon which her vision falls are all aglow with historic interest. A university so situated must be blind indeed if it does not recognize its obligations reverently to study the past in order that it may faithfully serve the present, and courageously trust the future. For in the past are to be found the origins of things, of nations, of institutions, of customs, of ideas, of beliefs, and a university that traces the development of these things through the ages must needs have much to say on the living questions of every age. This university, therefore, in our day must make itself a vital part of these times and of those that are to follow, by drawing out of its treasures things old and new. For if it be part of its mission to interpret to the present the meaning of the past, so it is equally a part of its duty to enlarge the life of the future by extending in every direction the boundaries of human knowledge.

A university that is set on a hill cannot be hid. I count it a matter of no little moment that here, in its new home, Columbia cannot escape the observation of the city, nor can the city escape from it. In the desire to be of service to the city, the university must ever find a potent inspiration. The university may not be indifferent to what is going on in the great city of which it is a part, and neither can the city forget, as it looks toward this hill, that there is in its midst in this university a life the great watchword of which is truth. The university by its very nature seeks first to learn the truth; then it seeks to teach the truth; and always it seeks to make men true to the truth they know. That is why, in my judgment, your college-bred men are so often idealists. The city may well cherish the university as one of the forces that make for its own ideal life.

It is no small part of the suitableness of this site for the uses of the university, that the university here will find itself in the inspiring presence of so many other forces that make for the uplifting of the city. If New York is taunted in the years to come with being a city wholly given up to the love of money, she may well point to this eminence with its cathedral, its hospital, its educational institutions, its monument to General Grant and say: "These are my jewels; these are the things my children care for more than they care for money—religion, philanthropy, education, patriotism; therefore, I wear these things in my civic crown." The cathedral will remind the university that "the heavens declare the glory of God and the firmament showeth his handiwork: that the earth also is the Lord's, and the fullness thereof;" that here, even in the midst of all this splendor, "we have no continuing city;" so that the university as it questions the heavens and the earth for their secrets shall do so reverently,

and yet fearlessly, in the confident expectation of the fulfillment of the promise graven from the beginning on the College seal, "In Thy light shall we see light."

I ask you also to notice how fortunately the hospital stands between the cathedral and the university; for if the hospital acquires from the cathedral its motive, it derives from the university its power. Modern medicine, modern surgery, and modern sanitation are all the children of the university; so the hospital stands, it may well be hoped, as a type of the rich blessings that are in store for men, so that in the days to come science and religion in all things shall recognize each other as natural allies, without reserve.

Patriotism is represented on this plateau by the tomb of General Grant; and I am glad that the work of the university is to be done under the shadow of this monument. Here was a man who consecrated every power that he had to the preservation of his country on the dreadful field of war, and when the war was over, consecrated all the influence he had won at the head of our successful armies to the work of reuniting the country he had done so much to save. It was no accident that his remains were followed to the tomb by men whom he had led and by men whom he had fought. I could not wish for young Americans preparing themselves in this university for their life's work a finer inspiration for all the duties of citizenship than is to be gained in the contemplation of that silent monitor. And thus the university will do its work in its new home in the midst of all these ennobling influences, at once inspiring and being inspired. It is an interesting circumstance, I think, that the university is the central figure of the entire group; certainly not because education is entitled to dominate either religion or patriotism, but because education should so certainly serve both.

In order that the foundations of our new home may be laid deep in love of country, and in the hope that a patriotism that shall know neither fear nor reproach may always be characteristic of this university and of all connected with it, arrangements have been made to receive to-day from Lafayette Post, G. A. R., a national flag that was tendered to the university by the Post several years ago. It is the purpose of the Post to present to the university a handsome base and standard for the flag, but it is not possible as yet to give to these their proper places. The flag to be presented to-day will fly, therefore, from a temporary staff; but it will hallow the ground none the less, for it is the flag of our country. The ceremony of presenting the flag will now take place.

ADDRESS

By Rear-Admiral Mead, U. S. N.,

COMMANDER OF LAFAYETTE POST

Mr. President :

A S a soldier of the Grand Army of the Republic and Commander of Lafayette Post, named for that chivalric young Frenchman who crossed the seas to champion the cause of Freedom, I have been delegated by my comrades to present to the President and Trustees of Columbia University the flag of our country, to be hoisted at the staff erected by Lafayette Post in front of the Library building, where resting upon a granite and bronze support, typical of the enduring nature of the principles symbolized by the banner of the nation, there will be found on the pedestal in letters of bronze the charge to the students of Columbia to "love, cherish and defend it."

Mr. President, as I stand here in the presence of this great gathering of men renowned in law, literature, art, science and commerce, I cannot help regretting that instead of a professional man of the sword, our committee did not select one of my comrades known to possess the gift of eloquence. My words may seem feeble in comparison with those that might fall from the lips of one trained to the bar and schooled in the devices that move great bodies of men to uncontrollable emotion through the sublime gift of oratory. Yet I am consoled in the thought that the words I utter come from the depths of my heart and that what I say is the result of an experience as a practical defender of the honor of this flag we men of the sword hold so dear.

Why do soldiers and sailors of the Republic love their colors as men love life?

Why is this emblem of nationality so dear to the hearts of the soldiers and sailors of the Republic?

Because, sir, the flag is to us what the cross was to the Christian apostles, what the cross on the hilt of his sword was to the knightly crusader—the emblem of faith, confidence, love. The standard of a nation has ever been to men a most sacred thing, so sacred, indeed, that Holy Writ declares by the mouth of the great law-giver (Numbers ii., 2)—" And every man of the children of Israel shall pitch by his own standard with the ensign of his father's house." So sacred that the Roman soldier was sworn upon his standard, and it was a common thing for the Roman generals to cast the standard into the ranks of the enemy, knowing well that to every man of his legion that standard was so precious that the most desperate deeds of valor would be done to regain it.

And rivalling the ancients of the heroic age, tens of thousands of American soldiers and sailors have sealed their devotion to their colors with their life's blood, and the great loyal heart of this free people goes out in gratitude to them for it, and this great nation of seventy millions can forever be trusted to remember the men who uphold the honor of the Stars and Stripes, for loyalty to the colors, whether to victory or defeat, whether to life or unto death—these are the marks of the true believer. How great a crime, then, does that man commit who brings shame upon the flag, the emblem of his country—and how great is the glory of that man who reflects honor upon his flag, the symbol of the nation's honor!

One of the most beautiful legends in the history of Christianity is that which tells the story of Constantine's vision. How on the march to Rome, sore oppressed in mind with doubts and fears as to the issue of his bold adventure and half tempted to retrace his steps, suddenly at midday above the splendor of the sun, he saw in the heavens a fiery cross and beneath it in letters of flame, the immortal legend :

" By this sign—Conquer ! "

Who will gainsay the assertion that this glorious emblem of our nationality, the flag of the Union, is as much the sign of hope to us as the radiant vision was to the great Roman soldier ?

Look at it as it kisses the winds with graceful folds and tell me if it be not the *one*, true rallying mark for all honest hearts of whatever race or belief who own allegiance to this mighty Republic.

Look at its beautiful colors as they gleam in the splendor of the sun, the *white* symbolic of purity and honor, the *red* typical of the blood which has been shed and which will continue to be shed, if need be, in defence of the integrity and perpetuity of American institutions, and the *blue* with its silvery stars representing the great canopy of heaven under which the soldier of the Republic on the land toils on the weary march or bivouacs in the silence of the night, or the sailor on the broad expanse of ocean keeps his weary watch and vigil that the citizens of the Republic may rest secure, while over all He who watches over the destinies of this mighty nation of freemen, He in whose kindly Providence our forefathers implicitly trusted, neither slumbers nor sleeps.

And under this immortal banner men of all shades of political opinion, of all forms of religious belief, can rally for the eternal principles of Right, Justice and Liberty under law. Loyalty to the Stars and Stripes—loyalty to the flag of the nation—that is the creed of the American. Perish the thought that there may be found dissenters to this creed north, south, east or west.

Our flag is the flag of Peace—it stands for Peace and not for war. Wherever it goes it carries encouragement and cheer to races of men less favored than ourselves. It is everywhere a harbinger of hope to the oppressed. It stands for Liberty unsullied by wanton License—for Freedom to worship God "without let or hindrance"—for the equality of all men before the law—for the greatest good to the greatest number.

It is the flag of Peace, Progress and Prosperity—it is not the flag of selfish aggrandizement. It has been the symbol in battle of the justice of its cause, for I dare to assert that Americans have never waged unjust wars, and that, God helping them, they never will. It is the flag that in the most terrible civil war of modern times stood always for Morality and not Rapine, Mercy and not Ruthlessness, Magnanimity and not Revenge—oh, sir, the flag of a benign Providence itself, for it symbolizes Justice, Mercy and Unity under the stars of Heaven.

Then, sir, if my words be true, be diligent in season and out of season to charge your youth who enter these halls of learning to "love, cherish and defend it."

ADDRESS

By Seth Low, LL.D.

PRESIDENT OF THE UNIVERSITY

Commander and Comrades of Lafayette Post:

ON behalf of Columbia University, I accept with gratitude and pleasure the flag you have presented to us. That you propose to add to your gift a permanent base and staff for the flag is welcome; but well I know that in your thoughts, as in ours, the flag is the principal thing. In the defence of this flag and for what it means, sons of Harvard, of Yale, of Princeton, and of Columbia, and of all the sisterhood of American colleges, have " thrown away their lives like a flower."

In the name of the men of King's College who fought for the independence of the Colonies, and did so much to establish the Government of these United States; in the name of the men of Columbia College who in the War of 1812 and in the Mexican War fought under this flag in the country's quarrel; and in the name of the men of Columbia University who fought, as you fought, in the war for the preservation of the Union, and who helped to bring unscathed out of the storm of the war this glorious flag, I pledge you for this university that we shall " love, cherish, and defend it."

As we shall be ready, God helping us, to die for it, in case of need, so I trust we shall be ready to live for it, striving always to make the country over which it floats ever worthier to be loved.

> " Long as thine Art shall love true love,
>   Long as thy Science truth shall know,
> Long as thine Eagle harms no dove,
>   Long as thy Law by Law shall grow,
> Long as thy God is God above,
>   Thy brother every man below—
> So long, dear Land of all my love,
>   Thy name shall shine, thy fame shall glow ! "

THE LIBRARY AND LAW SCHOOL.
MADISON AVENUE AND FORTY-NINTH STREET

ADDRESS

By the Hon. Abram S. Hewitt, LL.D.

THIS occasion and these impressive ceremonies are intended to recognize the trinity of religion, learning and patriotism. It is
most fitting that such a conjunction should be celebrated on these
Morningside Heights, consecrated by the blood of heroes in a conflict
which first showed the ability of the Continental militia to hold their
own against trained British soldiers whose valor had been proved on
many a hard fought field. It is meet and right that the minis-
ters of the churches which were associated in the foundation of
King's College, and that the Bishop and other clergy of the noble
Cathedral which hard by is slowly rearing its majestic proportions
to Heaven, should lend to this occasion the benediction of their
presence and their prayers. It accords with the fitness of things
that the Presidents and Faculties of the great sister Institutions of
Learning, which are the pride of the closing, and the hope of the
coming century, are here to rejoice with Columbia in the day of
her rejoicing, and to renew with her the pledge to train up a free
people in the virtue and knowledge on which their liberties depend. It is well for the Governor and the Regents of the University
of the great State of New York, by whose wise and timely legislation
Columbia College was reorganized and endowed with an estate, which
enables it at this late day to realize the expectations of the far-seeing
legislators who declared that she was to become " the mother of a

university," to witness the fulfillment of the prophecy of the fathers, on a scale of grandeur beyond the dreams of the most sanguine friends of sound learning. But above all, the presence of the Mayor of New York and of the members of the Corporation, its aldermen and commonalty, in this great audience assembled, is proof of the deep and abiding interest which the city has in the final dwelling place of an institution which, as I shall hope to show, has contributed largely to its growth, is the most striking monument of its progress, and must be its guide in the development which promises to make it chief among the cities of the world.

Such a rare concurrence of piety, learning, wisdom and authority indicates that this occasion has a significance which demands and justifies an explanation, familiar as it must necessarily be to the students of history and to the friends of education, but necessary in order to comprehend the genesis and the mission of the new university, destined to radiate its influence for good in all time to come from these buildings which we are here to dedicate to the service of God and man. Let it be remembered, however, that we are here not to dedicate buildings alone, but also to dedicate to the responsibilities and duties of advancing civilization the wealth, the energies and the potentialities of the millions of men who will in the ages to come constitute the population gathered around this centre of light and learning.

It is well that these ceremonies have been inaugurated by unfurling the national flag, which is the emblem of the sovereignty of the people. In every clime and under every form of government the flag represents the principle of loyalty to the constituted authority. Patriotism is not peculiar to any land nor to any people, but is the property of humanity wherever organized society exists. But with us the flag has a special significance. It represents not merely love of country, but something more. It is not only the ensign of the whole people, but it is the evidence of the liberty of the citizen, without which the stars and stripes would be for him but a badge of slavery. We are accustomed to speak of our Government as an "indestructible union of indestructible States," and in one sense this is a true definition, but in a larger spirit the Republic is rather to be regarded as an aggregation of units, every one of which is an independent citizen with equal rights and correlative duties.

But whence is the citizen to derive his knowledge of the nature of his rights, and how is he to rise to the full measure of the performance of his duties? Political knowledge is not a natural endowment. It is the growth of painful experience, and the outcome of training through ages of effort and sacrifice. The history of the world is the record of its acquisition. In its range are included the lessons of every age and every nation. Heroes and saints, statesmen and demagogues, tyrants and traitors have alike made their contributions to its evolution. The silent masses of the people have suffered and died in order that humanity might at length achieve freedom. There is not a region on this great globe which has not made its mark upon the final record which we call civilization.

But among all the peoples of the world to none has the opportunity been so propitious for waging the conflict between right and wrong, for carrying on the struggle between ignorance and knowledge, as in this land of ours, which seems to have been reserved under the providence of God for settlement by men who were dominated by a single idea, for which they were prepared to sacrifice home and comfort and wealth and all that men usually hold dear. The idea of personal liberty, which elsewhere was an abstraction, was made a reality in a new land, and the only land in which no aristocracy had ever existed, and privilege was unknown. They were enthusiasts who came to a region where there were no prejudices to encounter, no abuses to overcome, no traditions to fetter the free spirit of man. While they claimed the right to worship God according to the dictates of conscience, they held this right always subordinated to the individual liberty of the citizen. In whatever else they may have differed among themselves or with their neighbors, civil liberty was never in question, and its rights were asserted whenever and wherever assailed by kings, governors or parliaments. They regarded liberty as an end, and not as a means. "To secure it, to enjoy it and to diffuse it was the main object of all their social arrangements and of all their political struggles. They held it to be the inalienable prerogative of man, which he had no right to barter away for himself, and still less for his children. It was a sacred deposit, and the love of it was the main instinct engraven in their hearts." These pioneers of freedom understood that without education liberty would perish from the land in which they had sought refuge. They were not numerous, but they were as prolific as they were earnest, self-reliant and independent. It is estimated that the three millions who inhabited the British colonies which joined in the Revolution were descended from less than one hundred thousand immigrants, nearly all of whom could read and write, and some of whom were very learned men and statesmen of the highest order. They realized the value and necessity of education in order to preserve the liberty which they sought in a new world, and which they were prepared to defend at the peril of life and fortune. Hence they founded schools and colleges, even before they had acquired the primary comforts of civilization. Whatever else their children might lack, they were to be instructed in the knowledge of their political rights and their religious duties. Hence from the first religion and education were the inseparable guardians of liberty, equality and property. These three primary elements of the social organization were never separated, and indeed never separable in the minds of the exceptional men who laid the foundations of the Republic upon the inalienable rights of man. They justly held that private property was the concrete expression of liberty, and that any interference with property was an attack upon individual liberty. They believed that all men had an equal right to acquire and hold property, but they recognized that this very equality of opportunity would necessarily involve inequalities of possession, due to capacity, thrift and energy. Thus were developed communities of freemen, in which each man was master of himself, equal to every other man before the law, and recognizing no claim upon his property to which he had not assented as the price of the maintenance of order and the dispensation of justice.

While the love of liberty and its dependence upon education were recognized in all of the thirteen colonies, Massachusetts founded Harvard College one hundred years, Connecticut founded Yale fifty years, and Virginia founded William and Mary sixty years before New York had made any provision for higher education. Her youth were thus forced (reluctantly, perhaps, but probably to their gain) to resort for education to these institutions, which were afterwards denounced by the enemies of freedom as "nests of sedition." It is provided in the will of the father of a patriot whose fame constitutes one of the chief glories of our College that his son should never "be sent to the colony of Connecticut for his education, lest he should imbibe in his youth that low craft and cunning which they disguise under the sanctified garb of religion."

And yet, to the cadet of a New York family, graduated at Yale, we owe the fundamental condition in the charter of King's College, granted in 1754, that no tests shall "exclude any person of any religious denomination whatever from equal liberty and advantages of education." Moreover, in the long and bitter controversy which preceded the granting of the charter, the principle was laid down for the first time in the colonies that it was the duty of the State to provide for the education of all its children, free from the control of sectarian religious influence. The ideas thus propounded by William Livingston, the statesman and patriot, have all been incorporated into the legislation of the several States of the Union, and at length in the new constitution of the State of New York it is made a fundamental provision that no public money shall ever be appropriated to any educational institution under the control of any religious denomination.

The delay in the establishment of an institution for higher learning in New York was due, however, not so much to indifference or to opposition, as to the extraordinary variety in the nationality and religious belief of its inhabitants. Unlike New England, it was not homogeneous in creed or in race. It is said that eighteen different languages were spoken in the colony, and there were certainly thirteen different churches in the City of New York prior to the Revolution. When, however, at length the College came to be chartered, the leading denominations were all represented in the Board of Trustees, and so far as instruction was concerned, unlike the colleges of New England, it was absolutely unsectarian. Nevertheless, King's College was the special care of the Church of England, and its site was the gift of Trinity Church upon condition that its President should always be a communicant of the Church of England. If, however, it were thus expected that its graduates would be less devoted to the principles of individual liberty and the right of self-government, its promoters made a grievous mistake, for in the controversies which were soon to ensue between the colonies and the mother country, there were no more earnest advocates of the doctrine inherited from their Dutch, as well as from their English ancestry, that taxation should not be imposed without consent and without representation. It was the lucid and cogent argument of these patriots which called forth the eloquent eulogium of the elder Pitt, that they occupied the very first rank among logicians and statesmen. Even the large land holders of the State of New York were on the side of free government. Between them and the patriots of New England in the long struggle for liberty and equality there was entire sympathy of feeling and harmony of action. The contest was conducted in the main by college-bred men in all the colonies, while in the rank and file of the army there was scarcely a man who had not received a good common-school education. The feeling of equality which thus prevailed universally was not without its draw-backs when it became necessary to introduce military discipline. Here, upon the very ground where we stand, it was complained that each soldier seemed to regard himself as responsible for the issue of the battle, and followed the dictates of his own judgment rather than the orders of his superior officer. Washington, after the conflict was over, gave expression to his annoyance by the issue of a general order which expressly enjoined the necessity of obeying orders without assuming to question their wisdom. Nowhere and at no time during the struggle for independence was the fundamental idea of political equality ever forgotten, and when success was finally achieved, in every document which has been preserved, the blessings of liberty are declared to be the end and object of all the sacrifices of life and fortune which the struggle involved.

In this struggle the sons of our College bore a conspicuous and noble share. They were in fact not many in number, but of unusual parts, and probably better trained in sound learning, especially in the classics, than their compatriots from the other colonies. The first President of the College, Samuel Johnson, was a man of great piety and learning, the friend and companion of Berkeley, and the correspondent of his illustrious namesake, the lexicographer. In view of what our College is now doing and what it hopes to accomplish, it may be well to put on record here the aims which Dr. Johnson proposed to himself in the conduct of the institution which he had undertaken to organize: " A serious, *virtuous and industrious* course of life being first provided for, it is further the design of this college to instruct and perfect the youth in the learned languages and in the arts of reasoning exactly, of writing correctly, and speaking eloquently ; and in the arts of numbering and measuring, of surveying and navigation, of geography and history, of husbandry, commerce and government ; and in the knowledge of all nature in the heavens above us and in the air, water and earth around us, and the various kinds of meteors, stones, mines and minerals, plants and animals, and of everything useful for the comfort, the convenience and elegance of life in the chief manufactures relating to any of these things. And finally to lead them from the study of nature to the knowledge of themselves and of the God of Nature and their duty to Him, themselves and one another, and everything that can contribute to their true happiness both here and hereafter." I think it will be conceded that if our University shall be able to cover this ground and to accomplish the results expected to be produced by the college course, no just criticism or complaint will ever be made by the most ardent friend of education.

Certain it is that the scheme outlined in the original circular was carefully followed for more than one hundred years, during which the standard of scholarship was always of a high order, and the cultivation of morality and honor was maintained as the primary object of education.

If, as I have said, the leaders in the struggle for independence were college-bred men, the foundation of the Government and the formation of the Constitution was pre-eminently their work. Of the fifty-five members of the Constitutional Convention of 1787 nine were graduates of Princeton, four of Yale, three of Harvard, two of Columbia, one of Pennsylvania, seven of William and Mary and six of foreign colleges. The small number from Columbia was due to the fact that New York sent but three delegates to the Convention, but its two sons, Alexander Hamilton and Gouverneur Morris, were with Madison, and afterwards with Jay, in the "Federalist," the very bulwarks of that instrument which is acknowledged to be the most wonderful and successful political achievement ever devised by the wit of man. It is a mistake, however, to suppose that the Constitution was the application of a preconceived theory of government. It was, in fact, only the deliberate and inevitable expression of the ideas and experience of a people who had settled in the wilderness in order to enjoy social and religious liberty. They had fought

INTERIOR OF THE LIBRARY
MADISON AVENUE AND FORTY-NINTH STREET

and suffered for individual liberty, for equality before the law, and for the rights of property which they would not permit to be diminished even by taxation for public purposes without their own consent. The Constitution aimed, therefore, to secure to the individual citizen the right to labor in his own way, security for the property thus acquired, and absolute equality before the law. The essence of the Constitution is to be found in the declaration that " No man shall be deprived of life, liberty or property without due process of law." To make this declaration effective, the States were prohibited from passing "any law impairing the validity of contracts." Inasmuch as all contracts relating to property are practically solvable in money, the right "to coin money and regulate the value thereof is reserved to the Federal Government, while the States are forbidden to make anything but gold or silver a legal tender for the payment of debts." A supreme and unique tribunal is created to protect the citizen in his rights of person and property, and a National Government established which deals directly with the individual citizen and guarantees him in the enjoyment of these fundamental rights. Thus the whole history of our people culminates in the fruition of the idea which led to the settlement of the country, produced the War of Independence and created the Constitution, the individual right to liberty and the equality of citizens before the law.

If the construction of the Constitution was thus a triumph of patriotism over what appeared to be insuperable difficulties, its ratification by the States was only achieved by memorable efforts of wisdom and statesmanship. The battle was really fought out in the State of New York, where Hamilton, Jay, Morris and Livingston, who were the sons of our alma mater, overcame the opposition of Clinton, whose sturdy patriotism and great services to the cause of liberty made him a formidable foe. While the decision was still in doubt the impatient people of this city determined to celebrate the ratification of the Constitution, which was secured by the adhesion of the State of New Hampshire before the New York Convention could be induced to act. In the procession, which was the first of many memorable celebrations of a similar character, the professors and students of Columbia College took a conspicuous part. On the banner under which they marched were inscribed the words: "Science and Liberty mutually support and adorn each other." The author of this legend (certainly not remarkable for classic grace) could by no possibility have anticipated the potentialities for New York which were involved in these simple words. Liberty was indeed secured by the Constitution just ratified, but science was in its cradle. The principle of gravitation had been discovered, and the composition of air and water had recently been disclosed, but the application of this knowledge had not yet been made in America. Not a single steam engine had been erected on the continent, and beyond the rude application of a few water powers, all forms of industry were still carried on by hand. But the country was a land of unbounded resources, and its inhabitants, animated by individual energy and protected by law, were well prepared to undertake the conquest of a continent, and to develop its possibilities of wealth. The free spirit of the nation was thus loosened at the very juncture when science entered upon the career of discovery and development which has crowded the nineteenth century with great achievements and produced a sum of wealth far exceeding all the results of the eighteen preceding centuries of the Christian era. No pen can describe, no imagination can conceive the material triumphs of which this generation has been the witness and the partaker.

The favorable geographical position of New York gave it the natural primacy in this development, and its sons were not slow to see and to take advantage of its opportunity. DeWitt Clinton, the first graduate of Columbia College after the Revolution, created the Erie Canal, by which the wealth of the great West was opened up and poured into the lap of New York. Robert R. Livingston (another graduate), the great Chancellor who administered to Washington the oath of office, recognizing the genius of Fulton, supplied the means which made steam navigation a success. John Stevens, an alumnus of Columbia College, gave us the railway and the screw propellor, which have revolutionized transportation by land and by sea and enabled us to feed the teeming millions of Europe. · Thus were supplied the stimulus which has made the century now closing a very carnival of enterprise, and an uninterrupted triumph of science and industry.

But in order that the results of genius and energy may be made beneficial to society, the protection afforded by government and by law must be assured. This work fell to the lot of James Kent, appointed in 1793 Professor of Law in Columbia College. His lectures to the students, afterwards expanded into his "Commentaries on American Law," have had a deeper and more lasting influence in the formation of the national character than any secular book of the century. The rapid growth of wealth tends to undermine that respect for the rights of property which were imbedded in the Constitution, and hence the timely exposition of the great Chancellor, followed, as it was, by the exhaustive commentaries of Mr. Justice Story, became the inspiration of the conservative legislation which has characterized all the States of the Union, and produced that respect for law which is the most striking trait of our people, and which preserved the Federal Union in its time of peril.

Enough has been said to show not only that Columbia College has thus contributed its full share to the creation of the free Government, which is our chief glory, but that in the marvellous material development which has taken place under its influence and protection, the achievements of her sons have been of transcendent value. They have certainly made New York the largest and richest city on the Western continent, with possibilities of progress which promise to make it the metropolis of the world. With this conclusion we might rest the case of Columbia College in the consciousness that her past is at least secure. But this occasion takes note of the past only as the pioneer of the present, and the promise of the future.

A nation is not great because it is rich, any more than a man is a hero because he is a millionaire. The question is not how much riches we have accumulated but what we are doing with them. Is this great store of wealth being used merely for the acquisition of more wealth, and for the satisfaction of material wants and pleasures, or does a fair share of it go to the gratification of the spiritual needs of humanity and for its elevation into a higher and purer atmosphere?

These questions cannot be answered without a few words upon the nature and origin of the wealth which we find concentrated in the City of New York. Broadly it may be stated to be of two kinds—the one altogether material, in the form of commodities, houses and other visible property in which the value is due to the expenditure of labor and skill upon raw material; the other element of wealth is invisible and conventional, but none the less possessing commercial value because the world is willing to pay for genius, taste, beauty and potential utility. The most important form of this invisible value resides in that increment in the selling price of land, which comes from the mere presence and aggregation of population. It is estimated that one-half of the assessed value of real estate in the City of New York is of this conventional nature. Its evolution in this country is phenomenal, and it goes on steadily advancing because of the unceasing growth in urban population. When the Government was founded about three per cent. of the people resided in towns. To-day over one-third of the nation is dwelling in cities containing more than ten thousand people. The land which then was unsalable and was often abandoned to the tax gatherer, has become a source of wealth even where no structures have ever been erected on its surface. This increase in value, not due to any effort on the part of the owner, inures under our system of property solely to his benefit. It could not be otherwise without violating the principle of individual liberty on which our political system is based. The law imposes no obligation upon this form of property except the payment of taxes according to a general and uniform rate upon all property. And yet there is a feeling in the public mind that value created by the general effort has in morals attached to it certain obligations of trust, which do not inhere in other property produced by the labor and capital employed in the walks of industry and of commerce. In the City of New York, where the unearned increment has been ·most marked and can be most easily studied, it is interesting to observe how under natural laws, without the intervention of legislation, a very large portion of this increase has already been devoted to public use. Most of the large estates which, at the time of the founding of the College, extended uninterruptedly from its site on Murray Street to the limits of Manhattan Island, have already passed from the families of their original owners, and are now distributed among the community at large. The exceptions are to-day mostly devoted to public uses. Thus the King's farm, under the ownership of Trinity Church, is altogether used for religious and charitable objects. The same statement holds good of the property of the Dutch Church, of the New York Hospital, of the Sailors' Snug Harbor, and largely of the Lenox estate. The City of New York is itself the greatest beneficiary of this principle, because it is the largest landholder within its limits, and possesses a·vast amount of other property, and of franchises incident to property, the proceeds of which all go into the public treasury. Its other possessions have been secured by taxes levied mainly on real estate, which by the rise in value has been enabled to stand the heavy assessments for streets, parks, school-houses and the other necessary adjuncts of municipal life. Careful investigation will, I am convinced, prove that the total amount, which may be fairly regarded as due to the unearned increment of real estate, is represented substantially by the aggregate value of the property devoted to the public use, either under the direct control of the municipality, or in the numerous public institutions administered by trustees for the general benefit. The unearned increment, therefore, so often the subject of inconsiderate denunciation, is rather to be regarded as the equivalent of outlays made in the public interest, and as the measure as well as the means of development into a higher municipal life, due to a healthy growth in civilization. While it may appear that in a few striking instances, an excessive proportion of this fund has been secured to private ownership, the opportunity thus afforded to intelligent and conscientious capitalists to execute works of great public utility, which might otherwise be impossible or too long deferred, more than compensates for any temporary drawbacks incident to the personal control of large possessions, subjected as they always must be to the salutary influence of public opinion.

But Columbia College is perhaps the most prominent example of the beneficent operation of the natural tendency by which the unearned increment sooner or later is devoted to the public welfare. Its original buildings were erected by the proceeds of two lotteries authorized by the State, and by modest contributions from the enlightened friends of education at home and abroad. Its site consisted of about six acres of land, the gift of Trinity Church, which held the King's farm in trust for the promotion of religion and learning. Its value in 1754 was estimated by President Johnson at $16,000. In 1814 the State of New York, desirous to rid itself of the burthen of the Botanic Garden (which had been founded by Dr. Hosack, one of the most enlightened sons of Columbia) transferred to the latter the fee of about sixteen acres of unproductive land in the vicinity of what is now 50th Street and Fifth Avenue, estimated at the time to be worth about $20,000. These parcels of land now constitute the source from which the permanent revenue of the institution is derived. They are estimated to be worth twelve millions of dollars, and yield at the present time an annual revenue of $400,000.

This property practically enables higher education to be supplied at about one-half the actual cost of its provision. Thus Columbia College is not merely a great educational agency in which New York takes special pride because it is the product and evidence of its growth, but it is also a standing monument to the wisdom of our political system, founded on individual liberty and the security of property.

While this process of incrementation was thus slowly but surely progressing, it must be conceded that Columbia College, in common with the other institutions of learning throughout the country, fell into a condition of comparative stagnation, in marked contrast with the activity in the material and industrial world. It continued, indeed, to perform its original work of educating Christian gentlemen—men, who, as Herodotus says, "could ride and shoot and tell the truth," and whose influence in the community tended to promote conservative action and to mitigate the demoralizing influence of the mere pursuit of wealth. The Trustees of the College, upon whose roll for a century appear the names of the foremost citizens of this State, were at no time insensible to the desirability of extending its educational advantages so as to bear some adequate proportion to the growth of the city in population and enterprise. In 1810, in accordance with an able report presented by Rufus King, in which the primary principle of all sound education was declared to be "the evolution of faculty and the formation of habit," changes were made in the curriculum and in the discipline of the institution, which, however, failed to enlarge the demand for its privileges. In 1854, when the old college site became available for revenue, a comprehensive university scheme was devised by a committee of the Trustees, chief among whom was Dr. Henry James Anderson (of sweet and precious memory to the alumni of his time) which was justly regarded as the beginning of a new era in the educational history of the United States. Although this scheme was not at the time made operative, it resulted in securing for Columbia College the services of President

Barnard, under whose enlightened administration the initial steps leading to the present university development were taken. There is nothing more touching in the long history of the College than the devotion by President Barnard of his modest fortune to the execution of the plans which he had never ceased to urge for university extension, and to which he had consecrated his life and given the results of his ripe experience and vast resources of learning.

But the efforts of the colleges everywhere, even if they had been endowed (as they were not) with ample means, would have failed in view of the fact that the demand for instruction in the liberal arts had actually fallen off in this country, in consequence of the diversion into industrial pursuits of the most promising and intelligent young men, to whom the rewards of business were more attractive than the delights of learning. It is a remarkable fact that from the beginning of the century down to the conclusion of the late Civil War, there was an actual decline in the number of students who graduated at the various colleges in proportion to the whole population. In other words, while the country was growing in wealth, the conservative influence of sound learning was steadily diminishing, with the depressing results which are manifest to-day in every department of public life, in the halls of legislation, and in the sensational character of the public press.

The natural balance between the ethical and material elements of civilization has thus been deranged, and in the City of New York this dislocation is far greater than in any other portion of the land, because there is a greater disparity of wealth on the one side and poverty on the other, due largely to the vast influx of foreigners, many of them illiterate, who have been landed chiefly in this port. While the general average of wealth has more than doubled in fifty years, indicating a vast improvement in the condition of the people at large, there has been a differentiation between the two extremes of the scale—the very poor and the very rich— without a precedent in the history of society, and accompanied by an

79

accumulation of disturbing questions which, unless wisely dealt with, threaten an aggravation of discontent dangerous to social order.

Perhaps the most conspicuous feature of the time is the remarkable manner in which competition, heretofore regarded as the prime element of progress, is being checked and curbed by the principle of association. We have been made very familiar by the great extension of corporations during the last half century, with the beneficent results which spring from associated action. But of late the principle of combination has taken on a new and strange development, under which corporations are associated together for the purpose of controlling production and regulating prices. Contemporaneous with this new development, and, indeed, anterior to it, combinations of workmen have been formed to regulate wages and to determine who shall be permitted to labor in the walks of industry. The individual liberty of the citizen has thus been attacked on the one hand by trusts, and on the other hand by trades unions with an exhibition of power which threatens its very existence, and which, if finally triumphant, would overthrow the fundamental principle upon which our free Government was founded.

The same tendency towards the restriction of the liberty of the citizen can be detected in our recent politics. We have been taught, and have always believed, that free government could only be based upon the representative system, and yet of late it is manifest that this system fails in its aims and its results. The representative is no longer the choice of the people, but is the product of elaborate machinery, managed by men who devote themselves to politics in order to gain a livelihood. The will of the people no longer finds expression except when it happens to accord with the interests of the leaders who have practically put universal suffrage into commission.

We have been accustomed to rely in this country upon the public press for guidance and for the dissemination of sound principles in morals and politics. Indeed, the press has been regarded as the very

HAMILTON HALL

MADISON AVENUE AND FORTY-NINTH STREET

palladium of liberty, and yet within our day sensationalism has largely taken the place of reasonable discussion, and far too many of the metropolitan newspapers seem to have substituted greed for love of truth, and profit for the dignity of leadership.

Foreign immigration, which during the earlier part of the century was encouraged as a necessary means of development, and which in fact has largely contributed to the rapid growth of the country, has become a dangerous element, because much of it is now illiterate and of a character not easily assimilated into the general mass of the people. The magnitude of the danger may be inferred from the fact that we have received 18,000,000 of foreigners in the last twenty-five years too many of whom are not in sympathy with our institutions, and cannot discharge the ordinary duties of the citizen. Again, the franchise has been diluted in the Southern States with illiteracy to such an extent as to compel objectionable methods of interference in order to preserve society from peril, if not from ruin. The rights and duties of the suffrage are therefore undergoing a new discussion, the outcome of which is involved in great uncertainty. It may be predicted, however, that if limitations shall be prescribed they are more likely to be imposed upon the rich than upon the poor.

Crime also is thought to be on the increase, and to grow faster than the population. This ominous exception to the general experience of civilized nations in modern times shows that there is a radical and dangerous defect in our social system, to which the serious attention of the legislators might well be transferred from the contentions of foreign nations, in which we have but a sentimental interest.

Another manifestation of the time is the frequent and extensive dislocation of labor in all branches of industry, by which numbers of deserving persons are suddenly deprived of the means of livelihood. This is no place to discuss how far this condition is due to unwise legislation, but the fact is to be noted that at no time in the history of the country has there been such general discontent among the working classes as there is to-day in the presence of superfluous wealth controlled by a small number of individuals.

Although these are indeed serious evils, fraught with great peril to our republican institutions, there is not one of them which would not yield to the magic touch of knowledge and patriotism. Beset with difficulty as the task may be, and novel as some of the problems unquestionably are, they are not more formidable than those which were successfully solved by the great men of the Revolution and the framers of the Constitution. In the great crisis of the Civil War, and in the work of the reconstruction of the Union, involving the restoration of a sound financial system, statesmen were found equal to the responsibilities they were compelled to carry. Even the disputed Presidential succession, in our own day, was decided in a spirit of patriotism which called forth the plaudits of the world.

While we strive to take courage from these proofs that the heart of the people is still sound, we are dismayed by the existence of a Congress which stands dazed by the complexities of the tariff, and is in doubt whether there is a standard of value. Under the operation of the new constitution expressly amended to secure for the State of New York a reform in the civil service, and to protect its citizens from the politicians, we are forced to recognize the supremacy of an autocrat unknown to the law, and holding no commission from the people.

These are depressing facts, which might well make us despair of the Republic if we could not detect in many quarters, and especially from the possessors of the great wealth, which is to some extent responsible for the decay of statesmanship, the evidence of a reaction as healthy as it is reassuring. Thoughtful men, everywhere and in every rank of society, have come to the conclusion that the main cause of the degeneration of which we complain, is to be found in lack of knowledge, not merely among the politicians, but among the people at large. Hence, there is a general demand for education, not such as suffices merely for the performance of the ordinary duties of life and the conduct of industrial enterprises, but of a higher order, plainly required for the successful administration of public affairs, and calculated to raise the standard of intelligence and morals.

The feeling is rapidly spreading that the time has come for a new and nobler civilization. A spiritual wave like that which produced the crusades, erected the cathedrals and the universities in the Middle Ages, or the later movement which culminated in the Renaissance and in the Reformation, is plainly in sight and ready to usher in the advent of the next century, when the question will be, not as in the eighteenth century, "What are the rights of man," or in the nineteenth century, "How these rights are to be made available for the production of wealth," but rather what is the duty of society in regard to the use of wealth which has thus been created.

Already we can see the effect of this coming movement. In the present generation there has been a sudden and wonderful outbreak among rich men to endow higher institutions of learning, which they instinctively recognize as the true saviours of society. Not only have large benefactions been made to the existing colleges by which Harvard and Yale and Princeton and Columbia have been converted into true universities, but new universities have been munificently endowed by Cornell, Johns Hopkins, Rockefeller and Stanford, thus perfecting the chain of higher learning from the Atlantic to the Pacific Ocean. The smaller colleges and the technical schools have not been overlooked in this avalanche of munificence, but its characteristic feature is the recognition that something higher and nobler is needed in order to save the coming century from the materializing influence of the great increase of wealth in the nineteenth century. It is a confession that the mere knowledge of facts is not sufficient for the elevation of character, but that the ethical and spiritual side of man's nature needs the nutriment which can only be supplied by scholars and teachers who devote their lives to the pursuit of truth without regard to its material rewards.

· These considerations, which are true of the country at large, apply with peculiar force to Columbia College, which in the nature of things must become the foremost university, of the foremost city, of the foremost State, of the foremost country in the world. What opportunity, what possibility, what duty is implied in these simple words? How the souls of its Faculty and its Trustees must be inspired by the greatness of the undertaking! Confided to their hands is a vast fund, contributed not by individuals, but the product solely of the growth of New York. They must and do recognize, therefore, that its first duty is to the city by whose progress it has been thus enriched.

A city is not great because it contains many dwellings and covers much territory. Its greatness does not consist in mere numbers and in commerce. Its eminence is determined by the character of its civilization and by its provision for the material, intellectual and spiritual wants of its citizens. Life, liberty and property must be secured, order maintained, and the law enforced. The best system and appliances of education must be provided for its children; there must be adequate means of recreation from infancy to old age; the young must be trained to habits of obedience and diligence; outlets must be provided for their physical energies, and the spectacle of young men growing up without occupation must be removed from the conscience of the community, which is violated when there is no opportunity to learn mechanical trades—the natural outlet for their physical and mental powers. The population must be properly housed, perfect sanitary conditions must prevail, the standard of living must be raised, and parks and pleasure grounds provided on a scale which will enable every dweller in the city to exclaim:

> " I care not, Fortune, what you me deny,
> You cannnot rob me of free Nature's grace."

Schools for commercial and technical education must be provided at night, so that artisans of talent and ambition may have the opportunity to develop natural capacity to its full extent ; the evil influence of demoralizing resorts must be counteracted by the opening of museums of art, science, and industry, so that the population may become familiar with the highest types of beauty and the results of genius ; free libraries and reading-rooms must be provided on a scale demanded by the intellectual wants of an intelligent population ; such provision should be made for the sick and poor that there will be no excuse for the presence in its avenues of tramps and beggars; its streets should be well paved and clean ; transit should be speedy and cheap, and, above all, the churches should be conducted in a spirit so liberal as not merely to cultivate the religious instincts of men, but to exert a spiritual influence upon the rising generation through social organizations intended to amuse, instruct and refine.

Such will be the great city of the future, and such a city New York will be if the Columbia University, whose new birth we celebrate to-day, shall be enabled to perform its mission as the teacher and exponent of the best results of civilization. It is evident, however, that New York is in a formative condition, and has not yet attained to the ideals of municipal excellence. It seemed to realize its imperial destiny when, in 1837, it introduced an adequate water supply. In 1854 it recognized its coming greatness by the creation of the Central Park ; it was an inspiration of municipal genius when the Museums of Art and Natural History were founded upon a basis which secured the co-operation of enlightened and munificent citizens in providing admirable collections in the buildings erected by the city. The same policy will now give to New York the great free library which has been rendered possible by the private beneficence of Astor, Lenox and Tilden, whose endowments should be devoted solely to the increase of its collections and the expenses of administration. In fulfillment of the great ideals which have thus been slowly developed the city is now preparing to expend vast sums on speedways, docks, new means of transit, new and better schools, small parks and play-grounds in the older and more crowded portions of the city, and in diversions of a healthful kind demanded for the comfort, recreation and elevation of the masses of the people. It need not be feared that too much money will be invested in this direction if the works are wisely planned and honestly executed. The lessons of the Civil War taught the people of this country that its resources are practically exhaustless when expenditures are made for the benefit of the whole community.

I have been moved to make this plea for individual liberty and private property, because Columbia College by its origin, its history and its traditions stands, and ought to stand for them as a sure defence; and from the unique manner in which its endowment has been pro-vided should be a perpetual inspiration for the highest development of municipal spirit, as lofty as that which, in the days of Pericles made Athens "the eye of Greece," and by a sublime exhibition of civic genius crowned its Acropolis with the peerless temple of the Goddess of Wisdom, before which the world still bows with admiring recognition. To educate the citizen, to place before him the high-est ideals of duty, and to stimulate him to the stern performance of the obligations which rest upon him as a partaker in mind, body and estate of the inestimable benefits of good government ought to be the chief aim of the University, which from this day will be the most conspicuous and powerful institution in this great city. Here will be treasured the best memories of unselfish sacrifice and heroic achieve-ment; here will be recorded all the failures as well as the triumphs of civic statesmanship; here social problems will be discussed and solved through its affiliated institutions, which will reach every house-hold and every citizen. The children in the kindergartens, the boys and girls in the schools, the workmen in the shops, the clerks in the marts of commerce, the merchants and the manufacturers in their offices, the professional men in their studies, all will come under its influence. The efforts of the community will thus be co-ordinated for progress and for evolution into a higher and better environment. Every agency for instruction, for culture and for refinement will be systematically employed in the development of a nobler civic life; and, above all, the wealth which has accumulated in this city by the joint association of its people, and to which every human being contributes by his industry, will come to be regarded as a sacred trust to be administered in the public interest for works of benefi-cence to all. The petty jealousies between the classes will steadily disappear, and it will be demonstrated that democracy and liberty are co-existing and inseparable factors in the largest and best development of civilization.

The Trustees of the College have shown themselves to be fully conscious at all times of the obligation which rests upon them in the administration of the great trust confided to their keeping. From the humble beginning in 1754 with seven students and two instruct-ors, with an income so modest for nearly a century as to limit the in-struction of the College to such branches as were necessary to educate Christian gentlemen, the College under the wise guidance of Presi-dent Barnard and President Low has been developed into a University which, during the last year gave instruction to nineteen hundred and seventy-three students, enlisted the services of two hundred and sixty-five teachers, and expended a revenue of over $750,000. It now undertakes to provide instruction in all departments of human learn-ing required for the highest development of modern life. The old academic training is preserved for those who wish to lay the founda-tions of a scholarly education, fitting them for the study of the learned professions or for the pursuit of a literary career. Its schools of science qualify the engineers who are to become the captains of mod-ern industry, or to pass their lives in the study of natural phenomena ; its school of medicine, with its affiliated hospitals in connection with which the names of Sloane, Vanderbilt and Kissam will ever be held in grateful remembrance, provides the best instruction for alleviating the physical sufferings of the race, and the sanitary knowledge necessary to prevent the spread of disease; its school of law graduates the men who are to protect, enlarge and defend the civil rights of a free people, and to develop jurists who will have the knowledge, courage and honesty to maintain the law and administer justice without fear and without favor.

But, above all, and crowning all, is the school of political science, whose province it is to investigate the principles of justice, the elementary conditions and customs of the social organization, and the history and the results of their influence in the development of civilization, and the progress of man from a state of barbarism to the infinite refinements and culture of modern life. Herein Columbia College has realized the ideals of Jefferson for the university to which he gave the ripe experience and the affectionate devotion of his old age. It has given effect to the hopes of Washington, who in his first message delivered to Congress in this city, in his correspondence and in his last will, gave voice to the purpose which was near his heart, of founding an institution in which the principles of free government might be taught to specially selected students, who would thus be qualified for public office in the same manner as the Academy at West Point educated officers for the military service of the country. Already in issues of great moment the influence of Columbia University has done much to dispel error, to promote a better understanding between nations, and to avoid complications which might otherwise have resulted in actual hostilities.

Such is the university which the Legislature of New York in 1784 foreshadowed, when it declared that Columbia College was to be the mother under whose fostering care the educational system of the State would be made worthy of the great people who had pledged every dollar of its property for the education of every child within its domain.

But, as it is with the city which has given birth and wealth to this chief monument of its prosperity and glory, so the University stands only upon the threshold of a great career. Already it has outgrown the provision which a decade ago was supposed to be adequate for all possible requirements. By the general concurrence of its Trustees, its Faculty and its Alumni, and with the approval of the city and of the State, it is to be transferred to these historic heights, surrounded by a vision of beauty which satisfies the ideals of the poet, the patriot and the scholar. Here, then, is to be forever the centre of the intellectual life of the city—the citadel of last defense against the perils of ignorance, of superstition and of false doctrine. Here, buttressed by the noblest cathedral of our age, by institutions of charity and learning, and especially by Barnard College, in which, if the rich people of New York do their duty, the women of the future will be admitted to equal educational privileges with their brothers, the University buildings will forever under the flag of freedom be an unassailable bulwark of sound learning, and the gateway to universal knowledge.

If, then, the University has a duty to the City which it is striving to perform, have the citizens of New York no corresponding duty to discharge in providing it with the halls and buildings in which this beneficent work is henceforth to be carried on? If its vast endowment is to be sacredly applied, as it should be, to defray the cost of instruction and administration, ought not the rich citizens of New York, whose wealth has been derived from the same source and by virtue of the same law of increment which has given to Columbia College this endowment, be emulous to apply their surplus riches to the building of the structures, and to the provision of the appliances for higher education on a scale adequate to meet the ever-increasing demands of modern civilization? Large gifts have already been made by the Alumni, by the Fayerweather estate and by public-spirited citizens for the purchase of the new site. Seth Low, its honored President, inspired by filial piety and by public spirit, has given the great sum of money required for the construction of the library, around which all the other departments of the University must necessarily be grouped. William C. Schermerhorn, the Chairman of its Board of Trustees, whose long life of usefulness in this city has only been equalled by his modesty, has set the example of appropriating a portion of one of the large fortunes which have been created by the growth of the city to the erection of a hall of physical science, whose developments day by day are awakening an astonished world to new possiblities of discovery tending to the prevention and cure of disease, the increase of the general welfare, and to the final triumph of mind over matter.

While these lines are being penned, another family, among whose members are distinguished graduates from Columbia, have provided the means for erecting the great building devoted to chemical science and art, which will for all time commemorate the source from which the prosperity of the descendants of Frederick Christian Havemeyer, has been derived. For the naming of the remaining halls to be constructed, there will undoubtedly be a generous rivalry among the families whose names are connected with the early history of New York, and whose descendants have been enriched by its growth. In this country patents of nobility are wisely prohibited, but a title to immortality is surely within the reach of those to whom the Trustees may finally award the privilege and the glory of erecting any one of these buildings. One College Hall, however, the Trustees have wisely reserved for the Alumni to build by contributions, large or small, as a memorial to the living and dead sons of Columbia, whose names shall be inscribed upon tablets to be placed in the great hall of the building. In the entire history of Columbia College the number of its graduates has not been large, but in point of character, ability, and achievement the roll of honor is illustrious. Hereafter, when the University shall number its sons by hundreds of thousands, every one of these early names will have an interest for future generations, especially when they suggest the ties of family and excite the pride of an honorable ancestry. In the coming competition which I foresee, it is to be hoped that the Trustees will be very cautious in admitting to the company of the immortals, whose names these great halls shall bear, any one which may not hereafter revive the memory of an honorable and useful career in the acquisition of fortune. Thus Columbia will stand not only for what is pure in thought and action, but will be a perpetual incentive to virtue, public spirit, noble aspirations and successful achievement.

Although our system of government was intended by its founders to restrain the democratic spirit from hasty action, nevertheless political power has been steadily transferred from the few to the many, until at length the will of the majority may be said to be supreme, except for the barriers which are provided by the Constitution of the United States, and by the conviction of the people that their own liberties depend upon the protection afforded to private property—the essence of individual liberty. There is therefore, in this country but little jealousy of great fortunes. The cry of the demagogue against their possession finds small sympathy in the masses of the people, who understand that these fortunes usually represent value which has not been taken from the general wealth, but has not infrequently been contributed to it by the energy, the enterprise and the sound judgment of their creators. The existence of great fortunes, however, gives a corresponding opportunity for usefulness. Fortunately, by the laws of Nature wealth can only be made productive to its owner by such uses as are productive to the community. If this were not so the general fund would cease to grow, and progress would come to a halt. Public opinion more and more demands that great fortunes should be administered in a large and liberal spirit. Otherwise their possessors fall into general and just contempt. Although the universities where sound economic doctrines will be taught and disseminated may be relied upon to prevent the practical confiscation of private property, the mental condition of that man who is willing to share in the beneficial results of this defense to which he makes no contribution is not to be envied.

The masses of the people have never demanded equality of fortune, and indeed understand it to be impossible; but they have always insisted, and will always insist upon equality of opportunity. With free schools and universal education, with opportunities for the youth of exceptional ability in the ranks of the rich or the poor to secure the benefits of the highest instruction, the approaches of communism need never be feared. Equality of opportunity insures the ultimate distribution of wealth upon just conditions and within reasonable · periods of time. If this were not so, society would be justified in demanding a reorganization upon more equitable lines. But this demand will not be made so long as provision exists for the general diffusion of knowledge, and the acquisition of that higher learning which is essential to the stability and development of civil institutions.

Social reforms never come from below. They originate in the trained intellect of scholars and in the inspirations of genius in an atmosphere favorable to their reception. Slowly but surely great ideas descend and penetrate the mass of the people. The current belief of to-day was the scientific discovery of yesterday, while the evil of one age is very often due to reforms instituted in a previous age, and yet the underlying principles of truth and justice never change. The guardianship of these principles resides in the higher institutions of learning, and their application to the changing conditions of society depends upon teachers and scholars who devote their lives to the investigation of truth, regardless of the material results of their labor.

In this country the democracy, whose power will never grow less, will tolerate no violation of its ideals. But these ideals may be either true or false. They may lead to the ruin of society, as they did in the French Revolution, or they may raise it to new standards of justice and happiness. The outcome will depend on how far the public will is guided by the knowledge of sound principles. This knowledge cannot be acquired in the common schools. Even if every child is instructed in the rudiments of education, the limitations of age and of the time which can be devoted to elementary learning, do not admit of the intellectual and moral training necessary in dealing with great questions of public policy. It is true that in rare instances men like Benjamin Franklin, Roger Sherman and George Washington, who were not college bred, appear upon the stage of public life and take their place among the leaders of thought and action. But they were men of great natural powers which had been developed by extraordinary opportunities and responsibilities in early life, serving thus to prove the rule that thorough training and large experience in public affairs are prerequisites to successful administration.

Upon the University, then, we must build the foundations of our municipal glory and greatness. It will not lack the means of usefulness, nor the opportunity of expanding its influence, when the rich men of our city realize the opportunity it affords for making the millions which they control fulfill the duty imposed by the possession of wealth, and by which alone its possession can be justified. If Liberty, Science, Property and Labor are to continue to work together in the future as in the past for the advancement of civilization, the institutions of higher learning must be extended to the limits of their possibilities. So far as the City of New York is concerned the Columbia University must be made the fountain-head of knowledge, the centre from which will flow the conservative and recuperative principles of social progress. In association with all other beneficent influences it must be made to reach every household and to come into touch with every citizen. Against its walls the waves of communism and anarchy will then beat in vain. The city which is its home will feel its influence in every profession, in the walks of business, in its public institutions, in the conduct of its churches, in the execution and administration of the great undertakings which will be demanded by its continued growth.   Its citizens will come to its halls for instruction, for guidance and for inspiration, and as they approach the portal of a higher municipal life, and are confirmed in nobler aims, they will feel the force of the prophetic motto of King's College, the mother of the Columbia University in the city of New York, " In lumine tuo videbimus lumen."

ADDRESS

By Charles W. Eliot, LL.D.

PRESIDENT OF HARVARD UNIVERSITY

ONLY six years ago, near the close of the festivities which marked the happy inauguration of President Low, I ventured to say that Columbia's sister universities ardently wished she might acquire, in the common interests of all learning and philanthropy, much greater endowments than she then possessed, and particularly might get grounds and buildings worthy of the principal seat of learning in this rich and splendid mart. The experience of other institutions seemed to me to indicate that the new buildings might best be obtained through gifts from rich and sagacious men of good will. In the short interval between that day and this, the combined influence and efforts of President, Trustees, Faculties and Alumni, and the shining example of President Low, have brought much to pass; and it is my privilege to-day to bring you the hearty congratulations of the sister universities on the acquisition of this spacious site, of these rising buildings, and of numerous important additions to the material and intellectual resources of the University. To the governors of universities which occupy hundreds of acres of land in comparatively open towns or cities, even this noble site seems to offer but a closely restricted number of opportunities for those public-spirited persons who may reasonably aspire to erect buildings for the University. These precious opportunities for doing some perpetual good will be seized upon by a fortunate few, who shall in this nick of time both feel the desire and possess the means to serve their kind in a rarely delightful and enduring way, the beneficence of which has neither drawback nor alloy.

I congratulate the city, too, that its chief University is to have here a setting commensurate with the worth of its intellectual and spiritual influence. No American community can profit so much from the presence of a strong and progressive university as can this great city, at once magnificent and squalid, majestic and ignoble; at once Freedom's pride and Freedom's reproach. Universities are no longer merely students of the past, meditative observers of the present, or critics at safe distance of the actual struggles and strifes of the working world. They are active participants in all the fundamental, progressive work of modern society. By spoken word, by pen and pencil, through laboratories, libraries and collections, through courts, churches, schools, charities and hospitals, they promote the forward movement of society and help to open its onward way. Columbia University, in its recent history, amply illustrates this truth; for it has contributed effectively to the advancement of architecture, pedagogy, economics, political science, sociology, chemistry, physics, engineering and biology, in all which subjects the City of New York and the country at large have interests of incalculable magnitude. Through their perennial interest in philosophy and ethics, and in sacred and profane literature and history, universities enlarge and sweeten the inherited conceptions of the age in regard to religion and family life, and bring about modifications of obstructive dogma and ritual in organized religion, and of outgrown customs and laws concerning the family. This service is a vital one, since religion, in the universal sense, and the domestic affections remain, through all governmental and instrumental changes, the supreme forces in human society.

The influence of Columbia, and of all well-conducted American universities, is sure to become stronger and stronger as time goes on.

Our free institutions are going to receive a great service from the universities they have fostered. Whenever just sentiments, widely diffused through the mass of the people, can furnish sufficient guidance to wise public action, right determinations by universal suffrage may be relied on. Questions concerning independence, union, personal liberty, and religious toleration turn on such sentiments, and will be wisely settled by the mass of the people. But when the judicious determination of a public policy depends on careful collection of facts, keen discrimination, sound reasoning, and sure foresight, our Republic must soon follow, as all other civilized governments already do, the advice of highly trained men, who have made themselves by long study and observation experts in the matter in hand. Questions of currency, taxation, education, and public health belong to that class of public questions which absolutely require for their satisfactory settlement the knowledge and trained judgment of experts and the only wise decision which universal suffrage can make upon them is the decision to abide by expert opinion. The more complicated and difficult the public business becomes, the more pressing the need of expert management; and soon any other management will be simply ruinous. Now the experts needed are going to be trained in the American universities which, like Columbia, maintain at large centres of population well-equipped schools for all the learned and scientific professions.

The sister universities hope and expect that the citizens of New York will pour riches at the feet of Columbia; but they know that however much New York may do for the University, Columbia will do a hundred-fold more for the City and the State through the multifarious services of her sons taught here to discharge well their duties to society.

PROCEEDINGS UPON
THE LAYING OF THE CORNER-STONE
OF THE LIBRARY

PROCEEDINGS UPON THE LAYING OF THE CORNER-STONE OF THE LIBRARY

DECEMBER 7, 1895

SERVICE
The Rev. George R. Van DeWater, D.D.
OFFICIATING

LAYING OF THE CORNER-STONE

In the presence of the following-named Trustees:

William C. Schermerhorn, *Chairman*, Joseph W. Harper, Charles A. Silliman, Gerard Beekman, President Low, Lenox Smith, John Crosby Brown, Rt. Rev. Henry C. Potter, D.D., William H. Draper, M.D., Rev. Marvin R. Vincent, D.D., Cornelius Vanderbilt, George G. Wheelock, M.D., Hermann H. Cammann, William G. Lathrop, Jr., and John B. Pine, *Clerk*.

ADDRESS

By SETH LOW, LL.D.

PRESIDENT OF THE UNIVERSITY

GENTLEMEN OF THE TRUSTEES, LADIES AND GENTLEMEN:

THIS corner-stone is now to be set in its place. I hope that this stone will remain where it is set for centuries, bearing impressive witness, so long as it shall stand, to the skill and faithfulness of the men who construct this building and to the genius of the architect who has designed it. I hope that the building to be placed upon this corner-stone will similarly endure, and be at all times a centre of illumination and power within the city and without it, anear and afar, and be, as long as it shall last, a memorial of Abiel Abbot Low, in loving memory of whom this building is being reared.

The corner-stone will now be laid.

After laying the stone, the President continued:

On behalf of the Trustees of Columbia College, and in their name, I declare that this corner-stone is now laid.

Bible and Book of Common Prayer.

Charter and Acts relating to the University.

Statutes of the College and By-laws of the Trustees.

Historical sketch of the University.

Historical sketch of the College of Physicians and Surgeons.

General Catalogue of Officers and Alumni.

Annual Catalogue of the University.

Annual Reports of the President and Finance Committee for 1895.

Printed Reports of the Committee on Site and the Committee on Buildings and Grounds.

President Low's letter presenting the Library, and Resolutions of the Trustees accepting the gift and expressing the thanks of the Board.

Engraved portrait of Mr. Abiel Abbot Low.

Views and description of the new site and Library.

Official bulletins of the University and publications edited by members of the Faculties, current numbers.

Newspapers of the day.

STEPHEN P. NASH

BISHOP LITTLEJOHN

BISHOP POTTER

JOSEPH W. HARPER

WILLIAM H. DRAPER, M.D.

TRUSTEES OF THE UNIVERSITY

ADDRESS

By the Rt. Rev. Henry C. Potter, D.D., LL.D.

Mr. Chairman, Members of the Board of Trustees, Ladies and Gentlemen, and Mr. President:

O N the site on which we are assembled this afternoon, one hundred and twenty years ago come next 16th of September, there occurred a distinct act of rebellion, which was afterward, in the history of the land and of what was then called the Revolution, described as the Battle of Harlem. We have, therefore, appropriately, a Rector of Harlem this afternoon as Chaplain. The Battle of the Buckwheat Field was the first occasion on which the troops of the rebels successfully resisted the British troops. I recall this fact, because, melancholy as it may seem, we inaugurate this proceeding with what, I suppose, must also be distinctly recognized as an act of rebellion. If the President of Columbia College had insisted on the exercise of his authority, I greatly apprehend that this act, in which we have just taken part, would have been dismissed without any function whatever, without even this modest assemblage, and without the presence of the Board of Trustees. I would, therefore, for my own part, express my grateful acknowledgment to the Chairman of the Board for insisting upon our coming here and making some formal recognition, however slight, of this work and of the gift for which it stands. How large it is I need not remind you. How large is destined to be its influence upon the future of the University, I am sure you will all recognize.

Let me recall another date. Nearly one hundred and forty years ago the corner-stone of Kings College was laid; and between 1756 and 1776, that College inaugurated its work and first began to make its influence felt. Between that date and this how vast are the changes that have come to pass! I am sure you will agree with me that it is becoming on an occasion of this kind to recall them, and to recall, too, a change which since then has occurred on this site, alike of pathetic and suggestive interest. I do not know whether it has occurred to others here that precisely four years ago to-day, the proposition was first presented to the Trustees of Columbia College to purchase this property from those who represented the Bloomingdale Insane Asylum. What was the change then instituted? It was this: That this site, which had been devoted for so long a time to the care of the insane, and to efforts for the restoration of dethroned reason, was chosen to be hereafter put to the service of the enlargement of the domain of the powers of that reason in all the wide realms of knowledge in which man is to be the searcher. For myself, I confess my abundant thankfulness that the Trustees of Columbia College were able to secure this site, and have determined to place here this important building as a part of that group which is to be one of the supreme ornaments of this city, and in which Religion, Learning and Humanity are to combine to form a noble trinity: The House of God—the Cathedral; the Home for the Sick—St. Luke's Hospital; these are here united to the House of the Student and the Scholar. Books are the story of the thoughts and lives of men, and here they are to be gathered for the enduring instruction of all lovers of the truth.

I know, and you know, how absolutely on this occasion I am denied any personal reference, particularly to the giver of this building and his services to Columbia; but, though I may not speak of him or of his work, I must congratulate him in your presence that this building is to commemorate the services and character of his father.   Many of us knew Mr. Abiel Abbot Low, and recognized the singular charm of his character, its simplicity, its incorruptible integrity, its high purpose—qualities that have made the name of merchant prince no unmeaning one in this community.   Mr. Low was indeed a merchant prince, not because of his great wealth, but because of the great way in which he used that wealth in relieving suffering, and for the good of his fellow-men ; and surely this Library will be an especially appropriate memorial of such a character and such a life, gathering in, as it will, the best in all literature, even as his ships ransacked the seas and gathered together the wealth of the world, to make it potent for the good of man.   I congratulate you and the citizens of New York that we have the privilege of coming here to witness the beginning of such a work ; and I know that you will suffer me to say for you to him whose gift it is, that we thank God that He put it in his heart to give it, and endowed him with the means and the wisdom to carry it to its noble completion.

BENEDICTION

www.ingramcontent.com/pod-product-compliance
Lightning Source LLC
Chambersburg PA
CBHW032150010726
47493CB00008BA/2648

*9 7 8 3 3 3 7 3 8 8 0 0 3 *